MW00398930

MAD LOVE

SLATEVIEW HIGH #3

EVA ASHWOOD

ONE

NOT ALL PRISONS are made of steel and concrete.

Some are made of the finest marble and expensive mahogany.

I sat in front of the mirror at my vanity, in a bedroom that felt cold and empty. The space seemed far too large and far too small at the same time, and my skin itched from the feeling of confinement.

The door wasn't locked.

There were no chains around my ankles.

Yet I was a prisoner as surely as if there had been.

I bit my lip, and the girl with delicate features and pale blonde hair in the mirror bit her lip too. She looked wan and exhausted, with circles under her eyes from too little sleep and too much stress.

She looked... hopeless.

It was easier for me to inspect the face of the pitiful girl in the mirror if I pretended she wasn't me. If I pretended this wasn't my life. And in a way, it *wasn't*. This wasn't a life I had agreed to or asked for. It was the life being thrust upon me by my parents—by my father.

I had spent weeks, months, trying to find a way to prove his innocence and get him out of prison. I had made bargains with people I wasn't quite sure I should trust in my pursuit of that single objective. And I'd been certain that if my father was given a second chance, a new lease on life, he would make different decisions. Better ones. That he would run his business empire with more care and honor, and that he would consider how his actions affected others. That he would strive to use his vast fortune and resources for *good*.

But I was wrong.

That may have been the worst error I've ever made in my seventeen years, and I honestly don't know what hurts worse —the fact that I've finally learned the true depths of human greed, or the fact that my father was the one to teach me that lesson.

My stomach churned, and I pressed a hand over it, dropping my gaze from the mirror. I couldn't look at myself anymore. Every time I did, I remembered another version of myself. One with eyes that sparkled and a smile that came readily to her lips. One who was wild and full of life.

One who loved three beautiful, dangerous boys.

She was still inside me, that version of myself. But I felt like every day, she became suffocated a little bit more. As if my parents were doing everything they could to snuff her out.

The trappings of this wealthy, luxurious life had once felt comfortable and right. It was all I'd ever known.

But now I knew something else. I knew what it was like to dance in a cold, empty warehouse to music played on an old boom box, with only the blood rushing through my veins and the press of three hot, solid bodies around me to keep warm.

I knew what it was like to fight. To laugh.

To love.

Only one of those things happened in this house, and even the fighting felt stifled and suffocated. My parents could barely be in the same room with each other anymore, and I was almost positive Dad knew about Mom's affair with Mark Jemison. But they wouldn't even fight about it properly. They just picked at each other, throwing little poison darts with their words, and pretended that life could go on as normal, even though nothing was how it had been before Dad's arrest.

He was trying to get it back though. To put everything back together and rebuild the shattered pieces of his life.

And the way he hoped to accomplish that was by selling me off.

Of course, no actual bill of sale would be written up. No money would change hands as I said my wedding vows.

But that didn't change the basic fact that I was being sold.

I would marry Barrett King in the summer after my graduation, and Dad would gain access to Sebastian King's vast network of money, power, and connections. My father insisted it was for the good of our entire family and told me

over and over again that it was my duty. My part to play in
our family's recovery.

Duty.

It was a word I had come to hate.

It was a word I'd been raised on, one I'd heard over and
over again as a little girl. I'd been given everything I could
ever want, but in some ways, none of it was mine. Because it
all came at a price.

And it was one I was no longer sure I was willing to pay.

Before my dark thoughts could spiral any lower, there
was a soft knock on the door.

Turning to look over my shoulder, I called out,
"Come in."

I wished like hell it would be Ava, the sweet woman
who'd been part of our house staff before Dad's arrest. But
my parents hadn't hired her back, even though they'd
replaced most of the staff they'd lost when the Feds had
come for Dad. I wasn't sure why, and Dad would never
tell me.

Had Ava refused to come back? Had she gotten another
position that she liked better?

It broke my heart to think that, but I could hardly blame
her for wanting to stay far away from this house. I wished I
could join her in fleeing, honestly.

The door opened slowly, and as it did, I realized it wasn't
one of the house staff at all.

It was Mom.

My body tensed instantly, my back straightening as my

jaw clenched. I didn't want to see her. Especially not right now.

It'd been less than a week since my father had informed me I was to marry Barrett King, and my engagement party was already set for this evening.

Of course, I was no longer naive enough to believe the party had anything to do with me. It was a chance for my mother and father to show off their new connections to all their wealthy friends, to prove that they were worthy of being in the circle of elites once more.

It was a show, just like everything else about this life.

"Cordelia, dear." Mom smiled, but it looked forced. "You should be getting ready. We'll need you downstairs in an hour. I know you said you don't feel comfortable having one of the servants help you anymore, but please let me send Poppy up. I have your outfit chosen and ready, and she can help you with your hair and makeup. You need to look your best."

I didn't make a move to start dressing. I just stared at her. The other thing that hurt almost as much as my father's decision to marry me off was the fact that my Mom had made absolutely no effort to stop it from happening. I had hoped that maybe she would understand. After all, she'd been there with me in the tiny house we had rented on the other side of Baltimore. She had lived that life with me—although unlike me, she had never found a way to make the best of it. She'd never made any kind of peace with it or found the beauty and joy in the ugliness.

All she'd done was sleep with Mark Jemison, a man she once would've considered too far beneath her to even speak to, in order to get back small scraps of what she'd lost.

"Cordelia, are you listening?"

Annoyance sounded in Mom's tone now, and she crossed to my closet, pulling out the dress she'd had made specifically for this event. It was beautiful, there was no denying that. But I had no desire to wear it.

"Why are you doing this?" I asked finally, my voice a soft rasp.

My mother looked up from her examination of the ornately detailed bodice of the dress. "I told you. You need to be ready in an hour. Less than that now."

"No." I slid the chair back and rose to my feet, my voice gaining strength. "Why are you doing *this*? Why are you letting Dad force me into a marriage you know I don't want? Why aren't you fighting for me? *Helping* me?"

The words came out in a rush. They'd been locked in my chest ever since Dad had told her of the arrangement, just a short while after he'd told me about it.

Mom's lips pursed. She drew in a deep breath and let it out on a sigh, then turned back to the closet and hung the dress up before facing me again.

"I *am* helping you, dear. You might not realize it yet, but this is for the best. This marriage to Barrett won't just secure our future, but yours as well. You'll never want for anything in your life."

"You don't know what I want."

There was a roughness to my voice now, as emotions I'd tried to keep contained for the past several days bubbled up to the surface like hot oil. My heart was a cracked and crumbling lump of clay in my chest, and I hadn't been able to bring myself to tell the Lost Boys any of this yet. I didn't know how to tell them, what to say, so I'd barely spoken to them at all since Dad had laid down his order.

And it was fucking killing me.

Mom shook her head, smiling at me indulgently like I was a child who couldn't understand a math problem. She crossed toward me, reaching out to squeeze my shoulder gently. The gesture was probably meant to be soothing, but it took all of my willpower not to pull away from her touch.

"I *do* know what you want," she told me. "And believe me, I know how you're feeling better than almost anyone else could. That's how I know this is the right thing for you. When I wasn't much older than you are now, I married your father. Of course, I had my doubts. That's only natural. But I made the right choice."

The lump of clay that was my heart seemed to swell in my chest, pressing painfully on my lungs and making it hard to breathe.

"You *understand*?" I finally shrugged off her touch, shaking my head vehemently. "How could you possibly understand? Don't you see what a hypocrite you're being? Your marriage to Dad is a total sham, a fucking lie! You don't love him. You cheated on him. You *abandoned* him the second he stopped being your meal ticket. And now you're encouraging me to lock myself into the same kind of loveless marriage you have? Just to 'secure my future'? That's bullshit, Mom! Can't you see that?"

Her hand moved so fast I didn't even see it coming.

A resounding slap made my head whip to one side as a startled gasp fell from my lips. Pain exploded through my cheek and stars danced before my eyes.

I swallowed hard, adrenaline surging through my system as I slowly blinked and straightened, my hand coming up to press against my hot, tender cheek.

Mom's eyes flashed with anger, and she leveled a finger at me. "Do not ever speak to me like that again, Cordelia. I don't know what happened to you while we were getting by in the ghetto, but it turned you into someone I don't even recognize."

I blinked, staring at her as blood rushed in my ears.

All my life, I'd been taught to obey. To go along with what I was told, to never argue or talk back. My mother had never slapped me before—because she'd had no reason to. I had never stepped a foot out of line, never raised my voice to my parents or challenged their authority.

But she was right about one thing.

My time at Slateview *had* changed me.

The anger simmering beneath my skin burst out of me in a rush, and instead of shrinking back in the face of Mom's imperious glare, I threw myself at her, hands flying.

She shrieked and stumbled back, raising her arms to protect her face as she called for help, her voice high and shrill with panic. I didn't stop, lashing out in a frenzy as we both went down, landing in a heap on the floor with me on top.

"Cordelia!" she screamed, latching onto my wrists. "What is the matter with you?"

I could've given her a long fucking list if I'd been in my right mind. But through the haze of helpless fury that turned the whole world red, I couldn't put together a single thought. I couldn't speak, couldn't stop. I could only struggle wildly against my captor.

Because in that moment, that's all this woman was to me.

Just as I wrenched my wrist free of her hold, strong arms closed around my waist, pulling me back.

"Cordelia!"

My father's tone was angry and commanding, and he was too strong for me to break free of his hold, no matter how hard I struggled.

I grunted and flailed in his arms, cursing him and my mother, speaking in half-formed sentences. I had slipped over the line at some point from poised, rational girl to feral animal, and I didn't know how to flip the switch back.

But my father did.

"Poppy. Quickly." I felt him jerk his head, and a second later, Poppy rushed over. The newest member of our house staff was a quiet woman with straight brown hair and a long neck, and her eyes grew wide as she approached.

She had a bottle of pills in her hand, and my struggles slowed as I watched her pop it open and spill one into her hand. I watched as if I were mesmerized as she handed it to my father, who released one arm from around me and took it, then held it up in front of my face.

"Take this, Cordelia. It will help you calm down."

My dead heart beat out a heavy rhythm in my chest, and my hand trembled, but I took the pill. I had never been hit by my mother before, and my father had never physically restrained me before. He wasn't a violent man, but he was a man used to getting what he wanted. I didn't want to find out what would happen if I didn't obey him in this.

I popped the pill into my mouth and swallowed it dry.

It tasted as bitter as it felt.

TWO

AN HOUR LATER, Mom came back upstairs to fetch me.

Poppy had stayed with me the entire time, arranging my hair in an elaborate style and doing my makeup before helping me slip into the dress mother had chosen.

It was a routine I was so accustomed to I knew it in my bones, and my body went through the motions even as my mind slowly sank into a thick, sludgy morass.

Every blink of my eyelids seemed to happen in slow motion, and I was strangely conscious of the edges of my periphery, as if I were peering through a window at the world around me.

Anger still sat heavy in my heart, but with the sedative clouding my mind, I couldn't quite *feel* it anymore.

It was there. I knew it was there. And I knew why it was there.

But it was as if it was no longer my own.

"Are you ready?"

Mom's voice was curt, anger simmering in her tone. She had a small pink line down the side of her cheek where one of my fingernails had scratched her, and I could tell she'd tried to cover it up with makeup. Poppy had put extra concealer on my cheekbone too, where a small bruise had formed from the stinging force of my mother's palm.

We would both be going downstairs with battle scars, wounds we had traded with each other—but as long as they were covered up, I supposed nobody would care.

"Yes." I nodded dully, then glanced over at Poppy.

She looked like she was trying to keep her expression carefully neutral, but she didn't quite succeed. I could see worry and horror in the tight lines of her face, and I wondered what she was thinking. Was she horrified *for* me? Or because of me?

My dulled mind wasn't in any kind of shape to even guess at the answer to that, so I let it drift out of my mind as I followed Mom down the hall. The hubbub of voices floated up to us before we even reached the stairs, and I was certain that the ballroom would be full of guests. Just like always, my arrival had been carefully timed and coordinated for the maximum effect, and the buzz of conversation faded as I descended the steps, looking for all the world like a queen.

Still on autopilot, I made my way through the gathered crowd, smiling and kissing cheeks and accepting congratulations. My mother's hand stayed on my elbow, a constant, silent warning not to step out of line. Maybe she was also trying to make sure I didn't stumble or weave as I walked—that I didn't do anything to give away the fact that at least half of me was missing right now, snuffed out by the drugs.

The half that remained was a dutiful daughter, a practiced hostess, and a perfect lady.

Minutes ticked by as the party wore on, but I could hardly tell. I wasn't sure if the whole thing was going by in a rush or dragging out endlessly, but when I caught sight of Barrett coming toward me, something inside my numb heart and mind tried to rouse itself. Tried to tear through the thick veil that'd been wrapped around me.

No.

No, this isn't right at all.

"Ah, there she is!"

Barrett beamed at me as he reached me. He had the same smarmy smile I remembered, and his father stood just behind him, an identical smile on his face. They both gave me appraising looks like I was a particularly valuable piece of art, but not like I was a person.

When Barrett leaned forward to press a kiss to my lips, I jerked in surprise, yanking my head back and to the side so that his lips brushed the shell of my ear. Even that slight touch was enough to make nausea roil my stomach and my skin prickle unpleasantly. Not just because of the touch itself, but because of what it meant—what it stood for.

No. This is all wrong.

I stepped back clumsily before he could try to kiss me

again, and my mother's hand tightened on my upper arm, her nails digging into my skin.

Warning me.

Barrett's eyebrows furrowed for a second, and he shot me a look that was much less pleased than the first one he'd given me. There was an assessing quality to it, as if he were sizing me up. As if he'd realized for the first time that I was a human being with agency, not just some prize to be bartered for and won.

And he didn't appear to like that realization one bit.

He gave me one last hard look, then slipped his own mask back on, turning to greet several prominent Baltimore businessmen who'd no doubt been invited by my father.

We barely spoke for the rest of the party, and after one more rebuffed attempt to kiss me, Barrett kept his distance entirely.

But that wouldn't be the end of it. I wasn't naive enough to believe that just because I had shown I had no interest in him, that would mean this thing was over. His father had a deal with my father, and that meant even *if* Barrett decided he had no interest in marrying someone who didn't even like him, it would make no difference.

Both of our fates were sealed.

Dad barely looked my way for the entire party, spending all of his time and energy schmoozing with people who had once been his equals. I heard him talking loudly at one point to a group of them about Barrett and me, and when he attributed our upcoming marriage to "young love," my stomach clenched uncomfortably.

By the time the party ended in the late evening, the sedative my parents had forced on me was beginning to wear off, and I could think a bit more clearly, although I felt strangely exhausted—as if I'd been in a half-sleep for the past several hours and my body desperately craved real sleep.

My mother only stopped hovering at my shoulder when the last guest stepped out the door, and the smile melted from her face as she turned away from me. The scratch mark on her cheek had faded already, but I had a feeling her anger about it would last much, much longer.

"I'm going upstairs," she said shortly, turning toward the curved staircase, her heels clicking over the floor. "The staff will clean up."

"I'll be up shortly, darling," Dad said, his tone almost warm. He was a better actor than Mom was, and I was only now beginning to realize what a dangerous thing that was.

Mom disappeared up the steps, and Dad turned to me, his expression serious and sincere.

"I watched you tonight, Cordelia." He sighed. "I know you don't like this arrangement, and you probably don't see the point in it. But believe me, there is one. The connections our entire family will gain from this marriage will be enough to put us back in good standing among our peers." He stepped forward, laying a heavy hand on my shoulder. "You'll be grateful for this one day, sweetheart. I'm sure of it."

With a soft smile, he turned and headed up the stairs after Mom.

I stood in the large, empty ballroom for several long moments, gazing at my lavish surroundings as if I'd never seen them before. My fingers plucked idly at the delicate, expensive fabric of my dress, and I dragged in a deep breath through my nose. Then I took a few steps toward the stairs before hesitating.

I had no desire to go back to my room right now. It felt too prison-like, too confining. The truth of the matter was, I was trapped by far more than just a set of walls, but I couldn't stand the thought of locking myself up in my room again.

Several servants were making their way around the ballroom, cleaning and clearing away empty glasses, but they moved about like ghosts, never looking directly at me and skirting out of my way like fish as I turned and strode across the large room.

It only made me feel more like a ghost myself, like someone who wasn't quite real. As if I could rail and scream and protest all I liked, but no one would hear me. No one would listen.

I needed to feel alive. I needed to feel my own skin again.

So I made my way through the massive house toward the pool house at the back, walking down the glass enclosed corridor that connected it to the rest of the house. The lights were on when I walked into the space with beautifully tiled floors, large windows lining one wall, and an Olympic-sized swimming pool. They were set on a timer, going on and off every day despite the fact that the only people who usually came in here were maintenance staff.

My parents never used the pool. They'd only gotten it built because several of their friends had installed pools, and they couldn't bear to be left behind in anything. But as soon as it'd been added to the house, they had both promptly forgotten about it.

Because they'd never really wanted it in the first place. They just hadn't wanted to lose.

I didn't use it often either, but it had become a place I knew I could go when I wanted guaranteed privacy and solitude. And that was exactly what I craved right now. Time alone to think. To try to get my mind to function again, to get rid of the last vestiges of numbness in my body and soul.

None of the house staff would come in here either—they were all busy with cleanup from the party—so I didn't even hesitate before reaching back to feel for the zipper of my dress and tugging it down. I let the soft material drop to the tiled floor, not even bothering to pick it up and drape it over a lounge chair before walking toward the water in my strapless bra and panties. The lawn outside the windows was mostly dark, with just a few perfectly placed lights illuminating the sculptures my mother had commissioned.

I stepped off the edge into the deep end of the pool and let myself sink toward the bottom for a moment, little bubbles escaping my nose as the silky water surrounded me. Then I flutter-kicked toward the surface, brushing my wet hair out of my eyes as my head popped out of the water.

The pool water was cool, and the feel of it against my skin was exactly what I needed. My head felt massively clearer already as I began to swim the length of the pool, my strokes easy and practiced from the many private lessons I'd had.

I was on my third lap when an awareness prickled across my skin, making goose bumps rise all over my body. My heart thudded unevenly in my chest as I stopped swimming, my feet touching down in the shallow end as my gaze swept around the room.

I was being watched. I was sure of it.

It was late in the evening, and the lights in the pool house were dim, casting shifting blue reflections over the walls. There was no one in the large space with me, but when my gaze shifted to the floor-to-ceiling windows that ran along one wall, my breath caught in my throat.

Three figures appeared like ghosts out of the darkness. One with brown hair and intense features, one broad-shouldered and bulky, with short blond hair, and one with dark hair and eyes and caramel skin.

The Lost Boys.

THREE

I STARED at them in shock, breath suspended in my lungs.

All three boys gazed back at me with unblinking eyes as they came to a stop outside one window, and for a moment, I was sure I was imagining things. Hallucinating. Dreaming them up because I had missed them so fucking much.

Before I could rouse myself from my stupor and climb out of the water, they moved toward the door at one end of the pool house that led to the backyard. I saw Misael pull something from his jacket pocket, and a second later I lost sight of them as they gathered around the door.

Then a soft *click* echoed around the silent space, and the door swung open.

A gust of cold winter air swept into the pool house, chilling my wet hair and skin, and then all three boys stepped inside, closing the door softly behind them. They moved as a single unit like they so often did, striding toward the edge of the pool as their gazes found me again.

My heart couldn't decide whether it wanted to gallop or stop beating entirely, so it thudded unevenly in my chest, an erratic rhythm that made me feel like I was dying.

They know.

I wasn't sure how they'd found out or who had told them —hell, maybe they'd picked up the gossip from Muse, the man who kept his finger on the pulse of both Baltimore's underworld and its elite.

But they knew.

They knew I was engaged to Barrett King.

My stomach tried to turn itself inside out at the realization, and fear warred with self-disgust in my soul. I knew how much they all hated my father, Bishop especially. When I first met them, they had despised and distrusted my entire family, including me.

That had changed. So much had changed between us in the months that I'd known them. I had distrusted and disliked them at first too, but slowly, all of that had faded into a barely remembered past. They had become my saviors, my lovers, the three people I cared about and trusted more than anyone else in the world.

And what must they think of me now?

I wished desperately that I'd had the courage to tell them what my father had done, that they at least could've heard the words from my mouth instead of a someone else's.

Would they think I had done this on purpose? That I had

chosen Barrett over them? That I was no better than my mother, using people when I needed them and discarding them when I no longer needed them? Throwing them away for something better.

Seconds ticked by, each painfully full, but none of the Lost Boys spoke. They just looked at me, their bodies tense and their faces unreadable.

And I couldn't fucking bear it.

"I didn't know!" I blurted out, my voice too loud for the quiet pool house. My skin was cold now that I wasn't moving, but I could hardly register the sensation as every fiber of my being focused on the three boys in front of me. "I didn't know. I don't want this. Please, you have to believe me. I don't want Barrett. I will never want him. I'm yours. I'm *yours*. You said I'm yours, and I always will be."

My words were coming out almost faster than my tongue could speak them, tripping and falling over each other in their rush to escape my mouth. I had to make them understand.

I shook my head adamantly, wrapping my arms around myself under the water, heedless of the fact that I was nearly naked. "I belong to you. No one else. Ever. I won't let this happen—I'll stop it somehow, I promise I will. I'll kill myself before I marry Barrett King."

The last words bounced off the tiled walls around us, and they seemed to shock the Lost Boys into motion. In an instant, all three of them had shucked their jackets and shoes and jumped into the pool with me, still fully dressed. They converged on me, surrounding me on all sides, their bodies pressed so close I was suspended between them.

"Don't say that, Coralee," Bishop growled, grabbing my chin with one calloused hand. His touch was rough, his voice rougher, and he tilted my head up to meet my gaze. "*Never* fucking say that. We'll figure everything else out, but your life —*you*—come first. Always. Never say that shit again."

"You think we'd want that?" Misael murmured, sounding tortured. "That we'd rather you die than be with us? That's some fucked up kinda shit, Cora. What kind of people would we be if that's what we wanted?"

The pain in his voice cracked my heart open, and I swore I could feel the poison that'd been welling inside it start to spill out. I dragged in a breath, their unique scents mixing with the smell of chlorine in my nostrils, and for the first time in days, I felt... whole.

A tear slipped down my check, and unlike the other two boys, Kace didn't even say anything. He just wrapped an arm around my waist and hauled me against his body, pressing his lips to mine in a kiss that nearly eviscerated me. Every nerve ending in my body lit up as the wet fabric of his clothes scratched against my bare skin. They hadn't even bothered to strip before they'd jumped in with me, in too much of a hurry to reach me to worry about something like that.

The thought made something warm bloom in my belly, and I clutched at Kace's shoulders, giving back as good as I was getting as I kissed him with a ferocity that matched his own.

When he finally tore his lips from mine, he crushed me to him, wrapping his arms around me in a bear hug so tight I could hardly breathe. Not that I minded. I wished he could hold me tighter than this even, that he could somehow fuse our bodies together the same way our souls were. That all three of the boys could keep me so close that no one would be able to rip me away from them.

"We fuckin' missed you, Cora," he murmured roughly. "We knew somethin' was wrong when you went quiet, but we didn't find out till today that—"

He didn't say the words, and I didn't want him to. I'd already said Barrett's name twice tonight, and that was two times too many, as far as I was concerned. For just this moment, this blissful, wild moment, I was with my boys again and everything was alright.

It wasn't. Not in the big picture.

Them being here didn't negate or undo the arranged marriage my father had set up.

But it gave me peace, and it gave me *hope*. My boys were here. They still trusted me. They still wanted me.

And for now, that was enough.

Bishop and Misael had stepped closer when Kace pulled me into the hug, and I could feel all three of them touching me, hands roaming my body, breath warming my chilled skin.

A fire flared inside me. The same one that always burned for these boys, flickering like a pilot light in my lower belly, just waiting for the spark to reignite the flame. My hands clawed at Kace's back as I moved against him, struggling against his hold on me so I could rise up on my tiptoes and kiss him. And as soon as he released me, I did just that, pressing my wet chest against his and devouring his mouth with greedy, hungry kisses.

He responded instantly, and I could feel him getting hard against me, his cock pressing into my stomach as his tongue slid against mine.

"Switch."

The word was barely more than a low growl from beside me, and the next thing I knew, I was being spun in Kace's arms. Before I could orient myself, Bishop's lips crashed into mine, and a whole new sensation tore through my body.

Fuck, I'd missed kissing him. I'd missed kissing all of them. I'd missed everything about them.

It hadn't even been a full week since I'd seen them last, when we'd spent the night at the warehouse, but it felt like it'd been eons. So much had happened since then that I felt desperate to reconnect with them, to reassure both myself and them that no matter what else happened, no matter what my father or Sebastian King said, one truth remained unalterable.

I. Was. Theirs.

Misael made a noise behind me, his hands tracing my body under the water, his touch demanding and possessive. Bishop deepened our kiss, scraping our teeth together as his tongue delved into my mouth again, then he pulled away. His lips were swollen, just like I was sure mine were, and his eyes had a predatory, wild look to them.

There was no one else in the world he would relinquish me to right now other than Misael or Kace. But as a testament to the strength of the bond the three boys shared, Bish was the one who turned me in the water, presenting me to his friend.

Misael cupped my face in his hands, and for a moment, he didn't kiss me at all. He just stared at me, his gaze so full of emotion it made my chest ache sweetly. Then he pressed his lips against mine and drank me in.

The rest of the world faded away as Misael kissed my lips and Bishop and Kace explored my body. The sounds of our heavy breaths and low moans mingled with the gentle rhythm of pool water slapping against the edges of the pool, and I vaguely realized that I was no longer cold at all. The bodies pressing against me were warm and solid, and my own blood was rushing so fast that all my limbs tingled with energy.

This was what I wanted.

It was all I wanted.

Forever.

"I'm yours," I whispered, the sound swallowed up by Misael's hot kisses. "I'm yours. I'm yours."

I repeated it over and over like a promise. Like a prayer. And every time I said it, I could physically feel the reaction from my three boys.

Their touch grew rougher, more demanding, their hands sliding beneath the fabric of my bra and panties before

Bishop unsnapped my bra and hurled the wet garment out of the pool with a growl.

My nipples hardened instantly in the water, and Kace's hands were on them a second later, sending little shocks of pleasure through me as he squeezed and massaged the aching flesh. Bishop's fingers delved beneath the waistband of my panties, and when his fingertips brushed my clit, I cried out into Misael's mouth.

None of them took my sound as a signal to stop what they were doing. In fact, their movements became more urgent, more frantic as their breathing picked up. I could feel Bish's cock against my ass, and I ground against it, making a groan rumble in his chest.

"I..." My mouth wasn't working. My brain wasn't working. My lips were swollen and tingly, and I could barely stop kissing Misael long enough to speak. "I... need you."

For a moment, everything stopped. The boys gathered around me seemed to press even closer, encapsulating me between them until I could feel all three of their cocks pressing against me, separated from me only by their soaked clothes.

I could feel the tension in their bodies as they all seemed to privately war with themselves. And I knew why.

What we were doing was risky.

It was risky for them to even be here, for them to have stolen onto my family's property and broken into the pool house.

But giving in to the raw need coursing between us right now was even more dangerous.

I knew if I were being rational, I would be fighting against this, not begging for it. But rationality flew out the window around the same time Bishop had pulled my bra off. I needed to feel my skin against theirs.

Everywhere.

Pressing a kiss to the corner of Misael's mouth, I wedged my hand between us and stroked his length, even as my other hand found Kace's cock and I ground my ass against Bishop's hardness again.

"Please," I whispered.

And that one little word was all it took.

I didn't know if it was their own need overriding common sense just like mine had, or if they really would do anything I asked of them, but all three boys stepped back from me at once, tugging their sopping wet shirts over their heads. My greedy gaze took in the sight of their naked chests, and even though the water distorted their forms a little, it was the best thing I'd seen all week.

They tossed their shirts to the tiled floor beside the pool, and the wet garments landed with a dull *thwap*. I couldn't look away, my gaze flitting from one boy to the next as they each undid their pants, pushing the clinging fabric down until they could kick their pants all the way off. They deposited those by the side of the pool too, and suddenly, I was in the water with three very muscled, very naked boys.

My body temperature spiked, and a demanding ache

built between my thighs as we all looked at each other for a moment. Then a low whimper fell from my lips, and the tension snapped. They forged through the chest-deep water to converge on me again, and this time, bare skin brushed against bare skin as I was gathered into their embrace.

Hands and lips and teeth were everywhere, and somewhere in the middle of everything, my panties were torn from my body. The ruined garment sailed toward the edge of the pool too, but I didn't even see where it landed because at that moment, Bishop slid a thick finger inside me, and my head dropped back.

"Fuck. Yes," I muttered, grinding against the heel of his hand as he added a second finger and began to slide them in and out.

But it wasn't enough. I needed to re-seal the bond between us, to get as close to each of them as humanly possible.

"More. More."

My gasping words hardly made any sense, but I pressed against him as I spoke, hooking one leg around him and practically crawling up his body. Kace and Misael made low noises of approval as they helped me, lifting and supporting me until I was right where I wanted to be. My arms wrapped around Bishop's shoulders, and my legs went around his body as his fingers withdrew from my core and the head of his cock found my entrance.

We were all bathed in pool water, as wet as we could possibly be—but even so, I could tell I was soaked for him.

My arousal slicked his cock as he pressed inside me, and my toes curled as all the air rushed from my lungs.

I dropped my head to his shoulder, holding onto him as tightly as I could and devouring his wet skin with my lips and teeth as he used his grip on my hips to hold me steady as he fucked me.

I'd never done this in a pool before, and it felt good but strange, our movements slightly hampered by the resistance of the water around us. But it didn't stop Bishop from going hard and deep, and with every thrust, I felt him all over. He circled his hips a little every time he bottomed out inside me, grinding the base of his cock against my clit.

Sweet pressure was building up inside me, the pleasure that was radiating outward from my core only heightened by the lingering pain in my heart, by the wild confusion and helplessness that still clung to the edges of my mind.

It was a desperate fuck, for so many reasons.

Misael and Kace were right there with us, dropping kisses to my exposed skin and running their hands over my body. When Kace's hand dropped lower and squeezed one ass cheek in a bruising grip, I clenched around Bish, biting his shoulder to keep my cry muffled.

But Kace didn't stop there. As my entire body rocked with the force of Bishop's thrusts, he moved his hand over to my other cheek before slipping one finger between them. The thick digit found my tight hole, and when he pressed inside, my world exploded into fragments of pleasure. I came hard on Bishop's cock, gasping and whimpering as my core clamped around him. My ass clamped around Kace's finger too, as if I was trying to lock both boys inside me, to keep them there forever.

"Oh, fuck, you're tight," Bishop groaned, grabbing a fistful of my hair close to the roots and hauling my head up to kiss me hard. He kept driving into me even as I convulsed around him, and when Kace began to move his finger in a matching rhythm, I came again.

This time, it was too much for Bish. He followed me over the edge, his lips hot and demanding on mine as his cock throbbed inside me, his hips grinding against my clit.

Kace didn't stop moving his finger until the last aftershocks of the orgasm quaked through me, and I realized as he finally withdrew it that he had made it in past the second knuckle. That he'd been deeper inside me than I realized.

I groaned at the loss of him, and a moment later, I lost Bishop too as he pulled out of me. He kissed me one more time, his entire body relaxing under my touch, and lifted one hand out of the water to stroke my damp hair back from my face. His expression was peaceful, almost worshipful as he gazed at me with deep hazel eyes that seemed to glitter in the reflected light of the pool.

"Do you want more? Can you take all of us?"

I nodded, my heart hammering against my chest as excitement and need filled me. A smile quirked Bishop's lips, and he lifted me easily in the water, tugging me away from his body before turning me to face Misael. The boy with caramel skin welcomed me into his arms eagerly, and as my legs moved around him, I reached between us to wrap my fingers around his shaft.

He was thick and hard, and I could feel each ridge and vein under my fingertips as I stroked him. Then I stole a move I'd learned from Kace, brushing the tip of Misael's cock against my clit, using the broad, smooth head to tease us both.

"Oh shit, Cora."

His lips curled back in a grimace, his breath picking up as his hips jerked into my touch, just barely breaching my entrance.

And just like that, I was done teasing. I released my grip on him and tightened my legs, forcing myself closer to him and impaling myself on his length, and he groaned as he slid out and thrust in again.

I held onto him, resting my elbows on his shoulders and threading my hands through his hair. Then I looked back over my shoulder at Kace, biting my lip as my eyes urged him on with a silent invitation.

"Fuck yes, Princess," he growled, stepping up behind me again as his finger found my ass for the second time. This time, he worked his way in faster and matched his rhythm to Misael's, fucking me just like the boy in front of me was.

I'd never known this could be so good. I'd never known I would like it.

But I did.

My body did.

It must have, because I shattered around Misael after just

a few minutes, flailing for something to hold on to and finding Bishop's hand. He was standing a little off to one side, watching us with hooded eyes, and I squeezed his hand hard as I came, my body spasming in Misael's grasp as my core and ass clenched rhythmically. Kace left his finger inside me as deep as it would go, and the feeling of fullness was indescribable.

He circled it as he withdrew it, stretching out the tight muscles even more. Then his lips found my ear, brushing over the shell as he murmured, "Someday I'll take that pretty ass, Coralee. I'll fuck you in that tight, dark hole until you come all over my cock. Would you like that?"

I moaned, shuddering and clinging to Misael and Bishop, and both boys chuckled as Misael pulled out of me, leaving me feeling suddenly bereft.

Kace didn't laugh though. His cock was like steel against my ass as he stepped closer, hot and hard, and he brandished it like a weapon as his breath caressed my ear again.

"Maybe someday I'll fuck your ass while Bish or Misael takes your sweet pussy. See how tight you feel when you're stuffed full of us. You think you could take us, Princess?"

His words were filthy, and I could feel a blush creeping up my face even as I nodded. "Yes. I could. I want to."

All three boys reacted to my words, and before I realized what was happening, I was hauled into Kace's arms. I expected him to slide right into me, but he didn't. Instead, he palmed my ass with both hands and carried me toward the ladder at the edge of the pool, the two other boys close behind him.

"Hold on to me," he murmured, and I clung to him as he hauled us out of the water. Cool air hit my bare skin, and a fresh new wave of sensations cascaded through me.

Bishop and Misael stayed close to us as Kace carried me over to one of the lounge chairs set near the wall and deposited my naked, dripping body on it. A thrill of fear and excitement ran through me as he crawled onto the lounge chair with me, his slim, muscled hips slipping between my thighs as his cock ran through my folds.

We weren't any more or less likely to get caught having sex on this chair than we had been in the water. But this felt more dangerous somehow, more exposed, and it only heightened my need for him.

He must've felt the same way, because he didn't hesitate another second. His cock found the entrance to my throbbing, swollen core, and he drove inside, filling me in one hard stroke. Outside of the water, with no resistance, he could fuck me as hard and fast as he wanted—and he did, slamming into me over and over as if he was trying to leave his mark on me permanently. To brand me as his.

Theirs.

My body was worn out by the overload of sensation, by taking each of them one after the other. But I never wanted him to stop. I wanted him to mark me. I wanted to feel all of them for days, to carry them with me long after this moment.

I wanted their cum inside me.

"Kace..." My voice was breathy and strained. "I'm gonna —oh, fuck, I'm gonna—"

My words were cut off as he dropped his head and kissed me, slanting his mouth over mine again and again as he slowed his strokes, circling his pelvis and grinding against my clit.

And I fell apart.

I clung tightly to him, squeezing his cock and rolling my hips, and I felt him follow me into bliss. His cock jerked and pulsed as his whole body shuddered, and I could feel our combined wetness leaking from me as he stroked roughly in and out a few more times, riding out the last waves of pleasure.

Then he braced his forearms on the chair, gazing down at me with moss-green eyes. Bishop and Misael had ended up on either side of the chair, and they each pressed kisses to my damp skin as I stared back up at Kace.

He nodded, seeming to read the question in my eyes, to know I needed reassurance.

"You're ours, Princess. You always will be. No matter fucking what."

FOUR

NO MATTER FUCKING WHAT.

Kace's words landed in my chest, jumpstarting my dying heart back to life. It wasn't a solution to the problems that faced us, but it was a promise nonetheless. A vow that I would never be alone. That I wouldn't have to face the future alone.

With reluctance, he pulled out of me, and each boy kissed me again before I padded over to the small room at one end of the pool house and grabbed towels for all of us. I couldn't help them with their wet clothes, but I could at least make sure they were able to towel off.

As I returned with a stack of fluffy white towels in my hands, my footsteps stuttered at sight of the three of them. They were sitting on the lounge chairs, completely naked, their cocks still semi-hard. They looked like apex predators lounging by a watering hole—confident, dangerous, and completely unashamed.

They didn't exactly fit in with the lavish luxury of the pool house. Instead, they seemed to dominate it, claiming it as their rightful place whether the rest of the world agreed or not.

They're beautiful.

The thought lodged in my mind, and I smiled softly to myself as I resumed walking toward them, my skin heating slightly at the feel of their attention on me.

"You're fuckin' gorgeous, Coralee." Misael grinned at me as I approached, accepting a towel as his heated gaze perused my body.

I leaned up onto my tiptoes to kiss him, resting my palm against his chest. They would have to leave soon. I knew it, and I was sure they knew it too. I could feel us all trying to brace ourselves for that moment, trying to prepare for our inevitable parting.

One more kiss, a little voice in my mind kept whispering. *Just one more kiss.*

But it would never be enough. Every kiss I stole just made me hungry for the next one, a need that seemed to build and grow the more I fed it.

After we had dried ourselves off a little, the boys gathered their wet clothes as I picked up my dress and slipped it back on. I went without both bra and panties, zipping the dress up before turning to look at my three boys. Their damp clothes clung to their muscled bodies, highlighting every line and angle, and I bit my bottom lip, desire welling inside me once again.

Bishop gave a low chuckle and tugged me into his arms, pressing me full-length against his wet body. I yelped as water seeped into my dress, chilling my skin, and he stole the sound from my mouth as he kissed me, nearly bending me backward as he took it deeper and deeper.

When he finally released me, the front of my gown had turned a darker color from the water it had absorbed, and I laughed as I looked down at myself.

Then Bishop's hand caught my chin, tilting my face up to meet his gaze. "It'll be alright, Cora. We'll figure something out. Don't lose hope, okay?"

I reached up to grab his hand, clinging to it as I nodded. "Can I see you again soon?"

"Princess, you can see us any fuckin' time you want." Kace turned my head to steal a kiss, and Misael followed suit.

Then, as if they knew they'd never leave if they didn't go now, all three of them turned and headed for the door, disappearing back into the night like shadows.

I stood in the empty pool house for several long minutes, staring out into the darkness of the back lawn until I was sure they were gone—that they'd gotten off the property safely. Then I gathered up my soaked, destroyed undergarments and threw them in the trash before heading upstairs. My hair smelled strongly of chlorine, and I could feel cum sliding down my thigh, but it was with reluctance that I stepped into the shower in my en suite bathroom.

Part of me didn't want to get clean.

The Lost Boys had made me dirty, and I wanted to stay dirty for them.

They had ruined me.

And I wanted to stay ruined.

AT SCHOOL ON MONDAY, I clung to memories of the boys' visit, relishing the pleasant soreness between my legs.

I focused on Bishop's command that I not lose hope, doing everything I could to obey. But it wasn't easy.

Once, the halls of Slateview High had felt threatening and foreign. Now the corridors of Highland Park Academy felt that way. I had been back in classes for three weeks, and instead of getting better, it had only gotten more difficult.

I didn't fit here anymore.

Everything was bright and polished, not a single thing out of place. From the outside, the school looked perfect. But like so many other things about my life, it was an illusion.

Several of my old "friends" had tried to welcome me back into the fold with open arms, claiming they had wanted to reach out to me after my dad's arrest but hadn't been allowed by their parents. I didn't buy those stories, and I wouldn't have cared even if they were true. As far as I was concerned, everyone from my previous life had shown their true colors when disaster struck my family. It had revealed the true depth of our friendship, which was about as deep as a two inch grave.

The three girls I'd considered my best friends before my life had spiraled off its axis, Caitlin Barrington, Felicia Prentice, and Allison Rhodes, were interested in rekindling our friendship only in ways that benefitted them. I was a novelty around Highland Park now, and hanging out with me garnered them extra attention.

But that was the extent of it. None of them had any interest in learning what my life had truly been like while I'd been living in a part of Baltimore most of them had never even visited. None of them cared that I didn't want the marriage that would soon be forced on me.

None of them understood.

For the most part, I kept my head down at school and just tried to get by. My classes were much more difficult here than they had been at Slateview, where overworked and underpaid teachers had barely had the time or energy to hold their students to any kind of standard.

But as it turned out, keeping my head down was harder than I'd hoped.

As I walked through the halls after lunch period on my way to Chemistry, several girls I didn't know well stepped in front of me, blocking my path.

They were all juniors, and in all honesty, I hadn't paid

much attention to them when I'd been a student here before. The old Cora had been too involved with her elite circle of friends and her social obligations to pay attention to much else. Not that I'd been a bully—I'd just been enmeshed in my own world and hadn't ventured outside of it to make friends.

And by the expressions on their faces, none of these girls were looking to make friends either.

"Well, well. Look who it is. Little ghetto Cora, from the wrong side of the tracks," one of the girls crooned. Her red hair was stick straight, cascading over her shoulders like a silk ribbon, and her lips were twisted in a cruel smirk.

I grimaced. If they seriously thought a few taunting words were going to break me, they didn't know shit. After what I'd been through in the past several months, it would take a hell of a lot more than that to rattle me.

Rolling my eyes at the pack of mean girls, I moved to sidestep them. But as I did, the redheaded girl stepped into my way again. We almost collided as I stopped short, anger flaring inside me.

"You're not shit, Cordelia Van Rensselaer," she hissed. "We all know your daddy still deserves to be in prison. And now he's trying to pretend he's still fucking relevant when everybody in Baltimore knows what a piece of trash he really is. What trash your whole family is. He thinks marrying you off to a family that's actually got a decent pedigree will make a difference, but somebody needs to tell him that a polished piece of shit is still shit."

Acid sloshed in my stomach, and something white-hot poured through my veins like molten metal.

It wasn't her jabs against my father. It wasn't even her jabs against me. But the mention of my arranged marriage to Barrett, the fact that the ruination of my life was fodder for this bitch's entertainment?

No.

Fuck, no.

The thought had barely implanted in my brain before my body was moving. My fist drew back and flew forward so fast she never even saw the punch coming until it caught her on her left cheek, sending her stumbling backward.

Pain radiated up my arm like a jagged bolt of lightning, but just like it had after my mom had slapped me, rage filled my body with a feral sort of strength. Keeping my throbbing hand balled into a fist, I went after her again, sending the rest of the junior girls scattering like leaves in the wind as I caught the redhead on the jaw this time.

If we'd been at Slateview, no one would've interrupted the fight—except maybe the Lost Boys. They'd been the ones to maintain order in those halls, ruling by fear and keeping the peace by putting down anyone who overstepped.

But this wasn't Slateview.

Before I could even get a third hit in, several classroom doors burst open around us, and no fewer than three teachers rushed forward to pull me and the girl apart. I was panting and glaring at her, but the rage that'd flared faded enough for me to realize what I'd done, and I shook my hand out as Mr. Duprey, a political science teacher, glowered down at me.

"How about a visit to the dean, Ms. Van Rensselaer? Now."

The redheaded girl smirked at me, dabbing at her lips with her fingertips. She reminded me a little of Serena, the girl who'd gone out of her way to torture me at Slateview until the Lost Boys had taken me under their wing. Apparently, bitchiness was a personality trait that transcended wealth or social class.

"Yeah," I muttered. "Sure."

Mr. Duprey escorted me personally to the dean's office, and when the secretary ushered us inside, he explained that he'd caught me fighting in the halls.

Dean Clavier, an older man with a neatly trimmed beard and expensive, stylish glasses, nodded. "Thank you. I'll handle it."

As Mr. Duprey left, the dean waved at the chair in front of his desk, studying me carefully as I sat down. I didn't like the way he was looking at me—as if he thought he knew me. As if he thought he understood me.

He didn't. I was sure of that.

"Cordelia." He pressed his lips together, shaking his head slightly. "I wondered if I might be seeing you in my office. After everything you've been through, I can't say I'm all that surprised to see you acting out."

I gritted my teeth at his simplistic, condescending assumptions about my behavior, but kept silent.

He didn't seem to require a response anyway. Keeping a firm but patient expression fixed to his face, he continued.

"I know it must be quite a... culture shock to be coming back to our academy after spending a semester in a public school like Slateview. But I have to warn you, Ms. Van Rensselaer: what was acceptable at that institution will not fly here. There are rules that must be followed here, not the least of which is our insistence on decorum and non-violence. Hitting another student is a violation of everything Highland Park stands for."

I didn't bother telling him that there were plenty of things that happened inside these walls that went directly against what Highland Park "stood for," and when I still didn't speak, Dean Clavier leaned forward, resting his elbows on his desk and threading his fingers together.

"I know you've been adjusting to being back, so I'll let you go with a warning—*one* warning. That's all you'll get, and if this happens again, there will be very serious consequences that could affect your future at this institution. So bear that in mind next time you think about getting in a fight." He sighed, shaking his head. "I know you probably think of yourself as 'tough' and want to prove to everyone that you are. Street cred, I think you call it? But you're going to have to give that notion up if you want to continue to do well here."

I blinked at him, my face pulling into an unconscious grimace as I absorbed his words.

He was wrong. I didn't think of myself as tough, and I wasn't trying to prove anything to anyone.

I just wasn't afraid anymore. I was done following along blindly as decisions were made for me because I was scared to step out of line.

There was only one thing I truly feared now.

And I would do everything in my power to make sure it never came to pass.

FIVE

AFTER ENDURING a long and pointless lecture from Dean Clavier about the importance of maintaining my decorum and reputation, and about how I needed to think about my future, I was finally dismissed.

"You'll fit in here again soon enough, Cordelia," he said to me as I left, patting me on the shoulder as he ushered me out the door.

His words haunted me as I went through the rest of the day in a daze, clenching and unclenching my sore hand as I walked through the halls.

Maybe he was right. Maybe I would fit into this world again before long.

But did I *want* to?

No one else accosted me in the corridors, but word of my fight with the redhead—whose name I found out was Marissa —spread quickly through the school. By the end of the day

Caitlin, Felicia, and Allison had all seemed to decide association with me wasn't worth the potential damage to their social standing. None of them talked to me in our shared classes or even made eye contact with me in the halls.

My skin felt itchy and too-tight by the time I stepped through the doors into the cold January air.

I needed a break. An escape.

Digging my phone out of my bag, I pulled up Mom's contact and typed out a quick text to her.

ME: *I'm going to study with Caitlin, Felicia, and Allison. We might go see a movie afterward. I'll be home later.*

It was a flat out lie. None of those girls wanted to hang out with me, and the feeling was so mutual it was bordering on animosity. But I knew both of my parents had been worried about how I hadn't seemed to be reconnecting with my old friends, so I hoped that throwing their names out would make my mother less likely to give me a hard time.

A few people stared at me out of the corners of their eyes as I made my way across the parking lot full of luxury vehicles to the car my father had given me the day he'd announced my engagement to Barrett. I'd been tempted to throw the keys back in his face, since the whole thing felt like a bribe—but it was my only piece of freedom, so I had accepted it grudgingly.

Ignoring the looks and whispers, I climbed inside the Aston Martin and drove out of the parking lot, heading toward the only place I wanted to be right now.

As the cracked sidewalks and dirty buildings of my old

neighborhood came into view thirty minutes later, something seemed to loosen in my chest. I had never, ever thought this place might feel like home. But somehow, it did. And I missed it.

I didn't miss the squat little house I had shared with Mom that had been poorly insulated and always a little too cold. But I missed the memories that'd been formed there, the moments I'd had with the boys. I missed our Christmas celebration that had made the house feel like a home for the first time.

Bishop's house was right across the street, and when I pulled up outside, I saw his car parked in the driveway. The beat-up convertible with the top up was such a welcome sight that I practically leapt out of my car, slamming the door hard before hurrying up the walk. He technically lived with foster parents like the other two Lost Boys did, but his were almost never home. I was pretty sure they only fostered him for the money they received from the government—money Bish never saw a penny of.

He got by working for Nathaniel Ward, making his own way in the world rather than waiting for foster parents who didn't give a fuck to help him out in any way. I respected that, even though the work he and the other boys did had upset me at first. It wasn't always violent, but it was almost always illegal. Nathaniel Ward was a powerful crime lord in Baltimore's underground, and they'd been working for him for a while.

My hand was raised to rap on the door when it was

yanked open, and before I could even knock once, I was
pulled into Bishop's arms. Misael and Kace were in his living
room too, and they watched me with fond smiles as I sank
into Bishop's embrace.

"What the hell are you doin' here, Coralee?" he
murmured, his voice rumbling against my chest. "Why didn't
you tell us you were comin'? Is everything okay?"

"Yeah." I sucked in a deep lungful of his woodsy scent,
relishing in his masculine aroma. "Nothing's wrong. I just
wanted to see you."

"Well, we'll never complain about that." He released me,
grinning down at me. Then he grimaced. "But we were just
about to head out to meet Nathaniel."

"Why don't we bring her with?" Misael suggested.
"Nathaniel told us to bring her by again sometime,
remember? I think it's an open invitation."

I lit up, raising my eyebrows hopefully as I flicked my
gaze from Bish to Kace, hoping they'd both be on board with
that. Anything would be better than going home, and
although Nathaniel Ward still terrified me a little, I liked his
wife, Josephine.

Bishop and Kace exchanged a look, and I could tell they
were both weighing it carefully. What they'd said in the pool
house last night clearly hadn't been a lie. They put my safety
above everything else.

Finally, they both nodded and broke gazes. Kace ran a
hand through his short-cropped blond hair, the muscles of his
arm bunching and making the snake tattoo that wrapped

around it seem to move like it was alive. Despite the fact that it was the dead of winter, he was wearing a t-shirt and jeans which both hugged his large, muscled body.

"Yeah." He smiled at me, a rare and beautiful sight I had come to love. "Come with us, Coralee."

A few minutes later, the four of us piled into Bishop's car, and it felt so much like old times that something both pleasurable and painful pricked at my chest. I tried to tamp down the pain and focus only on the pleasure, repeating the words that Josephine had once said to me.

Appreciate what you have rather than worrying about what you might lose.

Right now, I had the Lost Boys, and they had me. And I was going to appreciate every minute I got to spend with them.

We listened to music and talked as we drove, and I could tell all of us felt the same giddy happiness at being together. The guys caught me up on what'd been going on at Slateview over the past week, and I told them about my run-in with Marissa.

Bishop shot me a sharp look when I mentioned that I'd punched her twice, and I didn't know if he was about to lecture me about keeping myself safe and not starting fights or pull the car over and yank me into his lap so he could fuck me. To my disappointment, he did neither, although heat reflected in his eyes as he lifted my hand from my lap and brought it to his lips, kissing my bruised knuckles.

Fire shot through my veins at the touch, and the car grew

quieter as we approached Nathaniel's house. Tension and desire filled the small space, and I had a strong feeling that if they hadn't been called for a meeting with him, they would've blown off every other responsibility and taken me back to Bishop's house to tear my clothes off.

When we arrived at the house, the man who looked like a butler greeted us. I'd been shocked the first time I had come here and seen how elegant and luxurious Nathaniel's house was, but it made much more sense to me now. The line between the criminal class and the elite class of Baltimore was razor thin, almost indistinguishable sometimes.

We were ushered upstairs to Nathaniel's office, and unlike the last time I'd been here, the people we passed by didn't look at us as if we had one foot in the grave already. A small shiver worked its way down my spine at the memory, and I felt the Lost Boys shift closer to me. I shot Misael a grateful glance, and he squeezed my hand.

The butler left us just outside Nathaniel's office, and when the man himself opened the door, his gaze traveled quickly over the boys before landing on me. I tensed slightly, not quite sure what his reaction would be, but he smiled broadly.

"Cora. It's nice to see you. How's everything been at home?"

There were more layers of subtext to that question than I could possibly untangle. It was because of Nathaniel's intervention that Dad had been proven innocent of the crimes he'd been accused of. Nathaniel had revealed that my father had been set up, and that revelation had resulted in his release from prison.

And in exchange, my father owed him a favor.

I hadn't forgotten about that bargain, and I was sure Nathaniel hadn't either. But his question didn't sound like it had been meant just as a reminder of the debt Dad owed him. He sounded genuinely curious, maybe even a little concerned—as if he had some idea what being wrenched out of this life and away from my boys had done to me.

"It's... it's been okay," I said, attempting to put on a smile. It was the vaguest answer I could give without outright lying, but he didn't seem fooled for one moment.

He cocked his head at me, then nodded, letting the subject drop. "Good. I'm glad to hear it. If you'd like to wait in the library while we deal with our business, I'll make sure Josephine knows you're here. I'm sure she'd love to say hello. I won't keep your boys for too long."

He gave me another smile and then ushered the Lost Boys into his office. Kace brushed his hand over my lower back as he stepped forward, the touch soothing and reassuring. Once they disappeared inside the office, I made my way toward the library. I'd gotten caught wandering in here by Josephine the first time I'd met her, but this time, I was actually hoping she would come and say hello.

There was something about her that drew me in, that made me want to listen when she spoke.

She was so different from my own mother, but was so many things I wanted to be.

She was soft without being weak. Elegant. Self-assured. She was a part of Nathaniel's world without allowing herself to become dominated by it, and I couldn't help but look to her as a role-model.

"Cora." Her smoky voice behind me made me turn, and a smile broke across my face as I caught sight of her. "What a pleasant surprise to see you here. I'm so glad you came with your boys today."

"Hi, Josephine."

She gestured me over to a seat by the window, glancing back toward the door as we settled down in the bright winter light streaming through the glass. "Nathaniel has been giving them greater and greater responsibility, and he's been quite pleased with their work. You should be proud."

I could tell she meant it, and it occurred to me that maybe Nathaniel was grooming the Lost Boys to step into higher level roles in his organization once they graduated high school. After all, it wouldn't be long now.

"That's good. I am," I said, surprising myself with how much I meant it.

There was a part of me that still resisted the idea of them becoming any more enmeshed in this life and this line of work. But at the same time, I had come to accept a long time ago that this was part of who they were. And it made me glad to see them succeeding.

"And how are you? How have things been?" Josephine asked, turning her attention back to me.

I opened my mouth to tell her the same thing I'd told

Nathaniel. That I was okay, and that things were fine. But somewhere between my brain and my tongue, the protective filter I had erected failed, and when my mouth finally did open, the truth spilled out.

"I'm engaged."

The two words felt like daggers to my own heart, and Josephine's eyes widened. Apparently, although the Lost Boys had gotten wind of it, the news hadn't reached Nathaniel yet—although I was sure it would now.

"You are?" she asked carefully, her gaze measuring my response as she spoke.

"Yes."

Before I could think or second-guess myself, I told her everything there was to know about the whole fucked up situation, every detail since my father had called me into his office to break the news to me. Her brows pulled together as I spoke, and when I finished, she was silent for a moment.

I waited, although I wasn't quite sure what I was waiting for. It wasn't like she could fix this.

No one could.

But I was still desperate to know her thoughts, to receive what little pittance of comfort she might be able to give me.

"My family no longer speaks to me," she said finally, and I blinked. That wasn't what I'd been expecting at all.

"They don't?"

"No." She shook her head, sadness entering her blue eyes. "They haven't since the day I married Nathaniel. I chose him over them, you see. And just as they had promised they would, they erased me from their lives."

My heart picked up its pace as I listened to her, leaning forward slightly as I hung on each word she uttered.

"Do you miss them?"

She smiled quietly, nodding. "Of course I do. But not as much as I used to. I love Nathaniel more than I've ever loved anyone in this world, and I've found a new family here. With him."

I tugged my lip between my teeth, considering her words. Could I do that? If it came down to it, if my father outright refused to let go of this insane marriage arrangement, could I walk away from him and my mother forever? Would he even let me?

Maybe Josephine could see a hint of the thoughts bouncing around inside my head, because she reached out, resting her hand over one of mine. "I'm not telling you this to send you off on some half-cocked mission. I know family and relationships are never simple or black-and-white. I know it can seem almost impossible to choose between duty and desire." She gave my hand a little squeeze. "So I suppose I'm just telling you this to let you know that I understand."

"Thank you."

My chin quivered, and I looked away quickly, willing myself not to cry. Josephine was a strong woman, and I wanted to show her that I was strong too. But her sympathy— her *empathy*—had hit me right in the chest, and I was more touched by it than I wanted to admit.

Before I could say anything else, voices in the hall outside interrupted us, and Josephine and I both looked up. She saw the look on my face, and a smile tilted her lips.

"Come on." She stood and inclined her head toward the door. "It sounds like your boys are ready for you."

SIX

AFTER WE LEFT Nathaniel's place, the boys drove me back to my car, and I reluctantly kissed them all goodbye before climbing inside. I was worried about Mom finding out that I hadn't actually gone anywhere with the girls from Highland Park, so I figured it was better to play things safe and get home quickly.

On the drive back across Baltimore, as I watched the houses around me grow larger and more luxurious, I thought about what Josephine had said.

Resolve grew in my chest like a block of steel.

I would find a way to stop this.

The first and most obvious place was with the other half of this marriage equation—Barrett King himself. He hadn't seemed particularly enthused about our planned wedding when I'd seen him at the engagement party, particularly not after my cold-as-ice reception of him.

Maybe he didn't want this either. And if he didn't, maybe I could recruit his help in talking our parents out of this. If both of us could present a united force, maybe Sebastian and my father would have to reconsider.

Normally, I made it a point to avoid Barrett at school, going out of my way to make sure our paths never crossed. But by Friday, I'd made up my mind.

I didn't head toward the cafeteria during my lunch period like usual. Instead, I made my way to the second floor of the school, hoping to catch him as he came out of his fourth period class. I arrived just after the class had let out, forging my way through the press of students heading in the opposite direction to peer into the classroom.

But he wasn't there.

Dammit. I must've been too slow.

I swiveled my head around, my gaze tracking over the people in the hallway. I caught a glimpse of a tall boy with dark hair disappearing into the library and perked up. He must be going to study. That was perfect. If I could catch him alone, it would be a lot easier to have this conversation.

After giving myself a few deep breaths to gather my thoughts, I walked toward the library and stepped inside. The large space was fairly empty since most people were at lunch, and I didn't see Barrett at any of the tables or chairs set up in the main area. I poked around in the stacks for a minute, then headed toward the small study rooms in the back of the library, set up so students could focus with fewer distractions.

When I stepped inside the first one, I froze, my jaw dropping open.

I'd found Barrett.

But he wasn't alone.

He had girl laid out over the large table in the middle of the room, her legs splayed wide as his hand moved beneath her skirt. His body was draped over hers, and he was sucking on her neck as she moaned and writhed beneath him.

For a second, I was too shocked to do more than stare at the sight in front of me, my mind struggling to comprehend what I was seeing.

Then a small noise fell from my lips, and the girl's eyes flew open. She yelped at the sight of me and slapped Barrett's back, drawing his attention away from her neck. He glanced up, and when his gaze followed her and landed on me, I could see his entire posture shift.

He stiffened, then dragged his hand out from beneath the girl's skirt, rising to stand straight as he did. He jerked his chin at her without saying a word, and she sat up and scooted off the table. Then she shot me an annoyed glare and left the room.

I blinked, staring dumbly at Barrett as he adjusted his blazer and crossed his arms over his chest, gazing back at me with a bland look on his face. When I didn't speak for a few more moments, he rolled his eyes.

"Do you need something, Cora? I presumed you did, or I wouldn't have sent Linsey away."

His tone was casual and languid, almost mocking, and it jerked me out of my stupor.

"What the *fuck* are you doing?" I demanded, my voice low and tight.

He cocked a brow at me. "Well, besides the fact that I think the answer to that is perfectly obvious, I don't feel I need to explain myself to you."

"But—" I sputtered, shock still resonating through me. "You were—"

"Yes, I'm well aware of what I was doing." The annoyance in his expression grew. "Do you have a point? Come on, Cora, it's not like I don't know you have someone on the side too."

I blinked. After my mom's infidelity over the past couple months, I'd had a knee-jerk reaction to the sight of Barrett kissing some girl in the library. But he was right, in a way. Except I had three someones, and they weren't "on the side" of anything, because I had never even dated Barrett. I had never wanted to be with him.

And if his hand up that girl's skirt was any indication, he had no interest in being with me either.

Maybe it's a good thing I found him like this.

Ignoring his open taunt about me seeing someone else, I licked my lips and stepped forward, my heart slamming against my ribs as hope welled in my chest. "So... you don't want this either? You don't want to get married?"

"What?" He pulled a face, looking at me like I was crazy.

"Well, you're not in love with me. I'm not in love with

you. We want other people. So does that mean you don't want to get married either?"

He still looked utterly baffled, and the annoyance was starting to creep into his expression again.

"What on earth does this have to do with the wedding?" he asked, gesturing around the small room as if to encompass everything that'd happened between him and Linsey in here.

"It has *everything* to do with the wedding," I blurted, my voice growing in pitch and volume. I couldn't understand what he was talking about.

"No, Cora. I think you've misunderstood this situation completely." He smirked, and there was a cruel edge to it that made my jaw clench. "Or did your father not explain to you fully that this is a marriage of *convenience*? As in, it would be convenient for our families to join their empires. That has nothing to do with who I choose to hook up with. I'm not interested in fidelity, you should know that right now." His gaze traced lightly up and down my body, and a mocking smile curved his lips. "Although we'll obviously be expected to produce an heir. That can be managed."

My stomach clenched so hard it felt like it was a black hole collapsing in on itself. I wrapped my arms around myself, unconsciously trying to block out his stare, to shield myself in some way.

"So you... you want to be married in name only? You don't care about me, but you *want* to go through with this?"

He shook his head, his brows furrowing as he took a step closer to me. "You seem so shocked by this concept, Cora. I'm a little surprised. Your time in the gutter must've really fucked with your head. Of course that's what I want. My family stands to gain a great deal from this marriage, and it's my duty to do what's best for the King line. You know who has the luxury of marrying based only on their *feelings?*" He twisted the word mockingly. "People who have nothing. Because they have nothing to lose."

His callous words and his languid attitude made me want to punch him, and my already bruised hand closed into a fist.

How could he want this? How could he see so clearly into our future, know exactly what this forced marriage would become, and still want it?

I didn't know.

But the one thing I was certain of was that Barrett King would never be my ally.

I opened my mouth, unsure of what to say, and finally realized there was nothing *to* say. Everything that needed to be said had been spoken already, and there was no point in wasting another fucking word on this boy. So I snapped my jaw shut and turned away.

He let out an annoyed huff as I stalked out of the room, and I had a sneaking suspicion he was pissed because he'd sent away his booty call just so we could have that short, pointless conversation.

A haze of anger filled my mind the rest of the day, and I went even farther out of my way than usual to avoid Barrett, certain that if I saw him again right now, I would lose my battle for self-control and end up punching his smug, smarmy face.

He wasn't the person I needed to talk to anyway.

Given what I'd just learned, given what I now knew, I needed to speak to my father.

I drove straight home as soon as classes let out and found Dad in his office. He'd always split his time between his home office and one in the business district of Baltimore, but he'd been working from home more since his release from prison. I assumed that would last until he felt like he'd fully recovered his standing among his peers, when he could lord his wealth and accomplishments over them again like he had for so long.

"Cora." He glanced up as I rapped on the door and pushed it open at the same time. He had left it ajar, his signal that it was okay to interrupt him if necessary.

And at the moment, it was very fucking necessary.

My heart thudded out an uneven rhythm in my chest as I crossed the room toward his desk.

"Barrett is cheating on me."

The atmosphere in the room seemed to shift with my words, and my father looked up from the papers he'd been going over, his eyes narrowing. "What?"

"I found him in a room in the library today with his hand up some girl's skirt."

My voice shook just a little as I spoke. This was way outside the kinds of things my father and I usually talked about, but he had to know. He was aware Mom had cheated on him, and he obviously wasn't as cavalier about it as Barrett had seemed to be about the idea of fidelity. So maybe, just maybe, hearing this would change his mind.

For a split second, I thought I had been right. His features hardened slightly, and his lips pressed into a thin line.

But then he shook his head, seeming to banish the tension that'd been gathering in his body. "This is hardly an appropriate conversation for a girl to have with her father, Cordelia."

I crossed my arms. "It is when the father is trying to force the girl to marry someone she doesn't love. Someone who straight-out *promised* her he would cheat on her."

"This is not my business. It's for you and Barrett to work out between yourselves. What happens between a husband and wife is no one's concern but theirs, and you will be his wife very soon."

"But, Dad—" I blurted, taking another step toward him as disbelief and anger burst inside my chest.

"Cordelia!"

His voice was like a whip, and I swore I could feel the sting of it across my skin. I froze, and my father rose from his chair slowly, planting his palms on his desk as his gaze bored into me.

"Do you think I'm not *aware*?" he asked, his voice low and hard. "Do you think I don't know what goes on under my own roof? That I don't know about your little guests in the pool house? There are surveillance systems in this house, Cordelia."

My blood seemed to freeze in my veins.

Fuck. Fuck, no.

I'd known there were security cameras placed around the property, both inside and outside the house. It was why I had been worried about the Lost Boys getting caught when they'd broken in. But all four of us had been too caught up in each other to be smart or rational, and all of us had overlooked the possibility that our actions in the pool house might be recorded.

By my father.

My stomach turned over, sending acid rushing up my throat. "Dad—I didn't—"

"I don't need an explanation," he said coolly, his gaze skating over my face as if he couldn't quite bear to look at me. "I erased the footage after what little I saw so that no one else could ever get their hands on it, since I refuse to let my daughter's indiscretions be used as blackmail against her. But you clearly think of yourself as an adult now, so from here on out, I will treat you as one. That means no more coddling. No more softening unpleasant realities of life to make them more palatable for you. You don't always get what you want, and it's high time you learned that."

His face remained carefully impassive, but I could hear rage simmering in his voice.

Shame tried to rise up in me, but it was overwhelmed by my anger and helplessness as I listened to my father's words. He didn't care if I cheated on Barrett, or if Barrett cheated on me. He didn't care that he was setting me up for a lifetime of unhappiness in a loveless marriage. He had made his decision, and he would stand by it like a stone sentinel no matter what.

"You're dismissed," he said, settling back into his chair and picking up the papers he'd set down as if we hadn't just had this conversation.

I gazed at him in shock for a moment, then forced my body into motion and turned to leave.

Just as I reached the door, his voice came from behind me again.

"Oh, and Cordelia? I didn't need your help to get out of prison. Things were well in hand before your meddling."

SEVEN

HE SHOULD STILL BE in prison.

My feet felt like lead as I walked away from my father's office, and that singular thought wouldn't leave my head. It burrowed into my mind like a tick, like a parasite, refusing to leave.

He should still be in prison.

I had spent weeks agonizing over the question of whether or not my father was guilty. Not just of the crimes for which he'd been arrested, but of being cruel and callous in business. He had openly admitted to making choices that had ruined the lives of people like Bishop's parents, but back when he'd been stuck behind bars—back when he'd still *needed* my help, as much as he might deny it now—he had promised me that he wanted to do better.

I could see that now for the lie it was, and it hurt my soul to know that I was seeing my father clearly for the first time.

With no artifice.

With none of his charm covering up his calculating nature.

I was seeing just how far he would go to get what he wanted. He'd always been willing to hurt strangers as he built his business empire, willing to sacrifice their happiness for his own. For his family's benefit.

And maybe he was convincing himself that this marriage arrangement was for all of us, that it was truly best for our whole family. But more and more, I believed that he was doing it only for himself.

He should still be in prison.

The thought made me sick. Josephine had been right when she'd acknowledged that nothing was ever simple or clear-cut when it came to family. Because even now, despite everything he'd done, there was a part of me who still hoped for redemption for my father. Who still held out a foolish belief that he might change, or that he might reveal he'd been a better person than I thought all along.

That there was a reason for all of this madness that actually made sense.

Tears blurred my vision as I made my way down the hall, heading for the door that led to the garage. My gut churned with horror at the idea of what my father had seen, that he *knew* about the Lost Boys. I'd been about to tell him about them when he had sprung the fact that I was engaged to Barrett on me, and ever since then, I'd been careful never to mention them.

Because my father was proving himself to be colder and more calculating than I had ever imagined possible. And if he knew how much those three boys meant to me, there was a very real possibility he would use it against me. That he would threaten them to gain my compliance.

I couldn't let that happen.

My heart fluttered in my chest like a panicked bird as I slid into my Aston Martin and pulled out of the garage. I had a sudden urge to hit the road and keep driving, to go as far and as fast as I could before my parents realized I was gone.

It felt like a noose was slowly closing around my neck, and I had the strange and terrifying feeling as I drove down the wide streets of our neighborhood that I was about to be locked away in a tower, never to be seen by the world again.

I drove blindly at first, not even paying attention to where I was going. And by the time I shook off the worst of my haze and paid attention to my surroundings, I was already headed across town.

Digging into my purse, I pulled out my phone and called Bishop, my hand shaking as I brought it to my ear. It rang twice before he answered, and I could hear the worry in his voice as he spoke.

"Hey, Princess. You okay?"

"No."

The single word burned my throat like glass, and I could practically feel the force of his concern through the phone.

"Where are you?"

I gave him the nearest cross street, and as soon as I finished, he spoke again.

"Are you safe?"

"Yes."

"Then pull over. Stay where you are. I'm out on an errand for Nathaniel, but I'll do it later. I'll be there in five."

I didn't bother to protest. I knew nothing I said would compel him to put his work above me, and the honest truth was, I needed to see him. My soul craved it, and my wrecked heart begged for it.

After pulling over onto a quiet side street, I waited, counting down the minutes. It only took four for Bishop to arrive. His car screeched around the corner and pulled to a stop beside mine, and he jerked his head, gesturing for me to get in.

I was already moving, gathering up my purse and shoving my door open. The second I slid into the passenger seat of his beat-up convertible, he gunned the engine again and took off down the street.

His entire body seemed tense, and I wasn't quite sure where he was taking us, but now that I was in his presence, I really didn't care where we went. He didn't press me to talk, just reached over and threaded his fingers through mine. A few minutes later, we pulled up to a spot near the water in a quiet, abandoned part of the city.

He shut the engine off and turned to face me in the gathering dusk. I wasn't quite sure why he hadn't just taken me back to his place, but I had a feeling it was because his foster parents were home for once.

"What happened, Cora?" he asked, his expression serious.

In a halting voice, I told him everything. As I spoke, I watched his expression shift, and a part of me wished I had never said anything.

But that wasn't who we were. That wasn't how our relationship functioned. I had learned that lesson after lying to him and the other Lost Boys about my search to find answers about my dad's setup and arrest. We were stronger as a team, and that team only worked when we were honest with each other.

When I finally finished speaking, the sun was all the way down, and light from the city behind us glistened on the water.

"I was wrong," I said quietly. "About all of it. And you were right. My father—he doesn't deserve to be free."

My gaze was fixed out the front windshield, and I wait for Bishop's words to come. For him to tell me I should've listened, or to blame me for freeing the man who had destroyed his family.

Tears leaked from my eyes and spilled down my cheeks, dropping from my chin. Everything Bishop might say to me, I had already said to myself a dozen times by now. And none of it was wrong.

But he didn't speak at all. Instead, his fingers came to rest under my chin, and he turned my face toward him. Then he pressed his lips to mine in the gentlest kiss he'd ever given me.

I didn't know how he knew that was exactly what I needed. Hell, *I* hadn't even known. But as his lips pressed tenderly to mine, some broken part of my heart seemed to heal over.

These past few months had been a fast and furious lesson in the harshness of the world and the horrible things people were capable of. I had tried to keep hope and optimism alive, but the conversation I'd had with my father today had broken something inside me.

And Bishop healed it.

With one sweet, soft kiss, he reminded me that I was loved. That there were people in this world who saw me for *me* and not just what they could take from me. How they could use me.

I fell into his kiss like it was the vast ocean before us, the entire world seeming to dissolve around me until nothing else existed but the press of his lips against mine, his calloused hand cupping my cheek, and the shared breath between us.

When he finally pulled away, it felt like he took a piece of my soul with him. But I didn't miss it at all, because he had left a piece of his with me.

His eyes bounced between mine, our faces still so close together our noses nearly brushed as he gazed at me.

"Coralee. I love you."

I felt the warmth of his breath against my skin as he

spoke, and my heart thudded hard and heavy against my ribs, every beat seeming to reverberate through my body.

The tears that had been falling before fell harder, pushed from my eyes by an overload of emotion that threatened to drown me.

"I love you too, Bishop," I choked out. "So much it hurts."

Maybe he was trying to heal my pain, or maybe he just couldn't bear having any space between us, but he leaned in and pressed his lips to mine again. He kept kissing me as he reached down to unbuckle my seatbelt, only pulling back long enough to move the strap out of the way. Then he was pulling me toward him, hauling my body across the center console until I straddled his lap.

He scooted the seat back, cursing softly into my mouth as the mechanism on the old car got stuck halfway. Then we both grappled for his seatbelt, our kiss becoming deeper, more frantic as our lips parted and our tongues slid against each other.

I could feel him growing hard against me, his cock grinding against my core where our bodies were pressed together by the tight confines of the car. I rocked against him, rubbing my clit against his firm length, giving pleasure and taking it at the same time. My hands found their way underneath his jacket, and I helped him awkwardly shrug it off. I'd been in too much of a hurry to put mine on when I'd left the house, and I was glad for it now. I wanted *less* between us, always—never more.

His large hands slid up my thighs, pushing my skirt up as

they went, and I cupped his face, breathing hard as his fingertips delved beneath the fabric of my panties.

"I love you, Bishop."

His cock jerked beneath me, straining toward me as his hips thrust upward.

"Say it again."

"I love you."

With a growl, he moved his hands around to my ass, dragging me even closer and making us both groan at the friction. "Again."

"I love you so fucking much."

He gave me a smile that was boyish and feral all at once, his teeth gleaming in the dim light from outside, and then his hands latched onto the soft fabric of my panties and ripped.

The flimsy garment shredded, and he tugged it away from my body as I flipped open the button of his pants and pulled down the zipper. When my fingertips brushed the velvet skin of his cock, he sucked in a breath. The tip was already wet with precum, and the feel of it sent a shock of arousal through me, making my core throb.

"Now, Cora," he grunted, grabbing my hips to help me rise over him in the awkward confines of the front seat. "I need to be inside you now."

I didn't make him wait. My hand fisted his thick, warm shaft, and I positioned myself over it and sank down, impaling myself fully.

"God, you're fuckin' gorgeous," he muttered, gazing at me with something like awe on his face.

He dropped his head, finding my neck with his lips and teeth, and his next words were spoken directly against my skin as he rocked up into me in small thrusts.

"Do you remember the first night I came to your house?"

"When you climbed in through my window?" I asked, a grin tilting my lips despite the overload of sensations raging through me. "Yeah."

"Do you know why I came?"

"Wasn't it to check out your new acquisition?" I asked, biting my lip as I began to ride him harder, rising up onto my knees before dropping back down on his cock.

He chuckled, and I could feel his body tense as he lifted his hips to meet mine, stroking in and out of me.

"No. I came to try to get you out of my system." He sounded almost tortured. "I should've known that would never be fucking possible."

One of his large hands stayed on my ass while the other moved up to grab a fistful of my hair close to the roots, using the grip to tilt my head back and giving him perfect access to my neck. He bit down on the soft skin there just as he thrust up hard into me once more, his cock pulsing inside me as he flooded me with his release.

My world dissolved into only pleasure and the slight sting of pain as I gripped him hard and followed him into oblivion.

EIGHT

AFTER I FINALLY CRAWLED OFF Bishop's lap and we cleaned ourselves up a bit, he drove me back to his neighborhood. He pulled up outside his house and peered at the darkened windows, then nodded at me.

"They're gone. Let's go."

His foster parents were nowhere to be found as we slipped inside the house. It was late evening, and I'd left the expensive new car my father had bought me in a part of Baltimore I didn't know all that well, but I couldn't bring myself to worry about it one bit. I didn't give a shit if it got jacked or stolen. And I was beyond caring if my Mom got suspicious when I texted her to tell her I was spending the night at Caitlin's house.

I didn't want to leave Bishop's presence right now, didn't want to leave the comforting bubble of love and desire that surrounded us.

We fell into bed together, and now that we were outside of the constraints of his car, he took his time worshipping my body, making me come twice with his hand and his mouth before sliding inside me. We fucked long and slow and deep until we were both breathless and covered in a sheen of sweat, and when he came with a low grunt, I followed him over the edge.

I could've fallen asleep easily afterward, but Bishop carried me into the shower and helped me clean up—and for once, I didn't care that the water in these old houses was never quite hot enough. His warm body surrounded mine, slick skin pressing against me as he lathered soap over me with possessive, greedy hands, making me feel perfectly cared for and content.

After we toweled off, we crawled under the covers together, and I draped myself over his chest like a cat, my legs tangling with his. He kissed my hair and murmured comforting words as sleep finally claimed me.

"OH, I see how it is. Nobody thought to call us for this little sleepover?"

I blinked awake at the teasing voice, catching sight of sunlight streaming through the windows of Bishop's bedroom.

He grunted beneath me, a sleepy sound, and I felt him stir as he woke up too.

We both turned to gaze at Misael and Kace, who stood just inside the bedroom doorway.

Misael had been the one to speak, and he winked when he caught my gaze, letting me know he'd just been teasing. I knew the guys didn't get jealous of the one-on-one time they each spent with me, especially since I had never shown preference or favoritism toward any one of them. How could I have, when I cared about them all equally? When my heart was bound to each of theirs just the same?

Still, I didn't like even the hint of him feeling left out, so I threw the covers off, making Bishop grumble good-naturedly, and traipsed across the room, completely unabashed at my nakedness. There was a time when I definitely would've been, but now I relished the hungry glint that came into Kace's and Misael's eyes as they watched me approach. I threw my arms around Misael's neck and kissed him soundly, rubbing my bare breasts against his chest as I did.

He reacted instantly, looping one arm around my waist to keep me close while the other roamed my body, sliding over the curve of my ass and squeezing.

"Oh, I see how it is…"

Kace's tone was teasing too as he mirrored Misael's words from earlier, and when I finally broke the kiss with the dark-haired boy, I stepped eagerly into Kace's arms, letting him claim my lips with his own. His tongue swept the seam of my mouth, and as soon as I opened for him, he took the kiss even deeper.

By the time we broke apart, I was breathing hard. It had

been meant to be just a sweet greeting, but as so often happened with these boys, my emotions had spiked beyond my control at just a touch. I could tell both of them felt it too, and when I glanced back over my shoulder at Bishop, I saw him watching me with heat and approval in his eyes.

He liked seeing me do this with his friends.

And I liked having him watch.

Misael groaned, sounding truly pained. "Dammit. Now all I want to do is crawl into bed and keep this goin'. But there's actually a reason we came by this morning." He glanced at Bishop. "Nathaniel needs us. He's got a job he needs taken care of."

Disappointment flooded me. I'd been completely on board with Misael's "crawl into bed" plan, and I wasn't ready to go back home yet. Hell, I wasn't sure I'd ever be ready. I was tempting fate by staying out so long—it was only a matter of time before my mother realized I hadn't actually reconnected with my old Highland Park friends. That I wasn't spending all of my free time with those stuck-up girls, but with three boys from the wrong side of the tracks.

But still, I couldn't keep myself from glancing around the room at each of the boys as I perked up a little. "Can I come again?"

Bishop smiled indulgently. He seemed a lot less nervous about the idea of me entering Nathaniel Ward's home than he once had, and a strange sort of pride rose in me at that thought. Somehow, against all odds, I had won the crime lord over. It probably helped a lot that his wife liked me, and

Nathaniel seemed head-over-heels in love with Josephine. I imagined there wasn't much in the entire world he *wouldn't* do for her.

"Alright, Princess. You can come."

The other two boys nodded in agreement, and I kissed Kace again, rising up onto my tiptoes before sauntering across the room to collect my clothes. All three of the Lost Boys groaned as they watched me, and I bit back a smile.

The butler didn't seem at all surprised to see me with the boys when we arrived at Nathaniel's house, and I realized that whether I had wanted to or not, I had become a part of this world.

That thought didn't scare me anywhere near as much as it once would have.

When we were brought to Nathaniel's study, I expected the older man would tell me to wait in the library like usual. I was actually hoping to have a chance to talk to Josephine. I hated to burden her with my troubles, but I wanted to ask her advice. Although I was actively trying not to think about it, the confrontation with my father in his office was weighing heavily on my mind. I felt like an animal in a trap that was slowly tightening around me, and I had no idea how to get out of it.

But instead of sending me off, Nathaniel waved me inside his study with the boys. I shot Bishop a questioning glance, but although his brows drew together, he nodded.

When the door closed behind us, Nathaniel strode around his desk to take his seat, picking up a half-smoked cigarette from the ashtray and taking a long pull before speaking.

"Have you three heard of Claudio Vega?" he asked.

All three boys shook their heads. I didn't even bother shaking mine, since I was almost positive the question hadn't been directed at me.

Nathaniel nodded, not looking surprised. "He's a new player on the scene. A lower level criminal who's been rising up the ranks and gaining more strength. He's not big enough to be a threat to me—yet. But he could be. So I'd like to cut off that possibility by bringing him into my fold now. I want to form an alliance with him to keep Luke Carmine in check."

I stood silently as all three boys reacted to that. I still wasn't quite sure why Nathaniel had wanted me to be here for this, since I certainly didn't know the ins and outs of the power struggles among the criminal organizations of Baltimore.

"Makes sense," Kace said. "So what do you need us to do?"

"I'd like you to start a conversation with Claudio. Pay him a visit and deliver a gift for me." He inclined his head toward me, a smile curving his lips. "Bring her with you. She won me over. Maybe she'll have the same effect on him."

I could feel the boys around me stiffen, but before any of them could speak, Nathaniel went on. He gave them instructions on exactly what message to deliver to Claudio, then pulled open a drawer in his desk and retrieved a small Manilla envelope.

"Give him this." He handed it to Misael. "I believe he'll appreciate it."

My gaze flicked to the small package. It looked innocuous enough, but I'd spent enough time in this world to know by now that its contents certainly weren't. Whether it was money or photographs or documents, it was certainly something that would benefit Claudio in some way.

"Okay," Kace said flatly. "That it?"

"Yes." Nathaniel nodded. "This isn't meant to be a grand overture. If we're going to form a worthwhile alliance, it will happen slowly. Let me know how it goes."

He dismissed us, and all four of us headed downstairs and back out to Bishop's waiting car. As soon as the last door closed and Bish cranked the engine, the tension I had felt gathering in all of them broke.

"Well." Misael huffed out a breath. "This is some bullshit."

"I know," Kace growled.

I glanced into the back seat at the two of them. "What? What's wrong with the assignment?"

"It's not the assignment they're pissed about, Princess," Bishop said quietly, reaching over to rest a hand on my leg. "It's the fact that Nathaniel is trying to use you as a bargaining tool now. We never should've brought you to his house in the first fucking place."

I blinked, considering his answer. It was true, I supposed. Nathaniel was using me. But for some reason, I didn't really mind. It occurred to me that even though we were leaving the house of one crime lord on our way to see another, I felt less anxious than I did every day I stepped through the doors of Highland Park Academy.

As if I belonged in this world more than my old one now.

"It's okay," I told them. "I want to go. Besides, you're just starting a conversation, right? It's a peaceful mission, so I shouldn't be in any danger."

Bishop's grip on my leg tightened, and although he didn't say anything to contradict my statement, I could feel the answer resounding through the car.

In this world, there was no such thing as guaranteed safety.

But that was the same in my old world too, wasn't it? The wealth and privilege of my social class was hardly more than an illusion of security—and that too could be ripped away at any moment. Personally, I'd rather live my life *without* the illusions. I'd rather see the danger and deal with it at face value.

We drove in tense silence to a nightclub on the west side of the city. It was barely noon when we pulled up outside, but it didn't matter that the club wasn't open yet. We weren't here for dancing anyway.

Kace led the way as we walked around to the side of the building, and when we reached a door at the back, we were allowed inside by two burly men with tattoos creeping up their necks from under the fabric of their shirts. They seemed less than impressed at the sight of us, but none of the Lost Boys appeared ruffled by that at all.

Bishop told them why we'd come and who we'd been sent by—and I watched the men's faces transform instantly. Although their reaction wasn't overt, I could tell that Nathaniel's name had just made all four of us a lot more worthy of attention. I just hoped it was the right kind of attention.

"Come with us."

One of the men jerked his head, leading us through the back hallways of the building until we reached the main part of the club. I had expected to find Claudio behind a desk like Nathaniel usually was, but instead, the two men led us toward a man standing behind the bar and pouring himself a drink.

He was younger than I'd expected, although maybe that made sense if he was an up-and-comer like Nathaniel had said. He had black hair and deeply tanned skin, and his arms were covered in tattoos too. He couldn't have been older than late-twenties or mid-thirties—or maybe it was just that he had a slightly boyish face.

Claudio looked up as we approached, raising his glass to his lips before looking at one of the men who'd escorted us.

The man answered without even needing to hear the question. "Nathaniel Ward sent them. They say they've got a gift and a message."

"Well, I love gifts." Claudio grinned broadly, jerking his head to gesture us all forward.

The boys all took a seat on the barstools facing Claudio, keeping me close to them and slightly behind them, as if trying to put their bodies between me and the small-time crime boss.

They needn't have bothered. Claudio's gaze passed over all of us, but his expression wasn't hostile. In fact, he looked curious more than anything.

The three boys launched into their explanation of why we were here. As he spoke, Misael reached across the bar and presented the small envelope Nathaniel had given him. Claudio cocked his head, studying Misael for a moment before taking the envelope. He ripped it open and peered inside, and his expression told me I'd been right—whatever was in there was worth a lot to him.

Finally, he looked back up at all of us, picking up his drink again and taking another sip.

"Tell Nathanial 'thank you.' I'm not willin' to make any promises at this point, but I'd be open to discussing an alliance with him. I'll need to think about it." His gaze traveled over all of us again, then he nodded decisively. "Come back and see me again in a few weeks. We'll talk more then."

NINE

I COULDN'T TELL if "we'll talk more then" was a good thing or a bad thing, but the boys seemed satisfied with it. They shot the shit with Claudio for several more minutes, although I noticed that after the initial conversation, everyone was careful to steer the conversation *away* from business. The business part would be important later, but for the moment, it was just two different factions of Baltimore's underground getting to know each other.

The boys seemed to have relaxed a bit by the time we left, and I assumed that meant they considered their mission a success.

Reluctantly, Bishop pulled onto the freeway and cut across the city to where I'd parked my car the previous evening. I kissed each boy goodbye until we were all breathless and panting again, then finally pushed open my door and climbed out.

I didn't know how it was possible, but every time I said goodbye to the Lost Boys, it got harder and harder. My heart ached as I watched Bish's car pull away down the street and round the corner, and I swore I had left three pieces of it in the beat-up convertible with them.

My lips pressed together as I started the Aston Martin. The silence and emptiness inside the car seemed oppressive, so I cranked up the radio as I drove, trying to fill the space with something. When I pulled into the large garage and cut the engine, the sudden quiet seemed to echo around me, and I shook off a sudden wave of unease as I got out and walked toward the house.

It was mid-afternoon by now, and I passed several members of the house staff, who shot me cursory glances before looking away. I was sure all of them could feel the tension throbbing under the surface in this house, and they all seemed to have resolved to do everything they could to keep their heads down and ignore it.

I understood that impulse. My father could be an intimidating man, and he held their fates in his hands. They were probably worried about being in the wrong place at the wrong time and bearing the brunt of his anger, even if they weren't the ones who deserved it.

Keeping my footsteps light, I made my way through the great room on the first floor, heading for the stairs on the other side. But before I could reach them, voices in the distance caught my attention. The low sounds were coming from the direction of Dad's office, and I slowed my steps as I craned my head to listen.

"...shouldn't let her stay out all night."

That was my father's voice. His words were clipped, and annoyance filled his tone.

"She's finally spending time with her friends again. I thought you wanted that. After all, if she picks up her friendships with those girls, maybe their parents will finally take you back into their fold again," Mom said sharply.

"That's not necessary. I've got everything in hand. What I don't need—what we don't need—is to have Cordelia thinking she can go wherever she wants and do whatever she pleases. She's been spending far too much time out of the house lately."

"She's still adjusting," Mom murmured.

I would've been grateful for her defense of me if I didn't think she was saying it more to defend herself. After all, she'd been the one I had texted when I'd gone out with the boys the last two times, not Dad. And I'd chosen her for a reason.

"She's had enough time for that. She's back home now. Things are back to normal. And it's high time she started acting like it."

My father's voice was firm, the kind of tone that left no room for argument. I didn't stick around long enough to find out if Mom argued back anyway. Staying on the balls of my feet, I darted across the remainder of the great room and up the stairs, not stopping until I reached my bedroom.

Fuck. I'd been right to worry about staying out so much.

My parents were beginning to get suspicious.

I DIDN'T SEE the Lost Boys at all for the next two weeks. We texted every day, and I clung to those short messages like a lifeline, but it barely felt like enough.

Dad didn't seem to know that I'd gone to spend time with the Lost Boys when I'd stayed out all night. Like my mother, he believed I'd been at a sleepover with my old friends from Highland Park.

But it didn't change the fact that he knew about the boys' visit to our house, and what we'd done in the pool house.

And it didn't change the fact that he was now watching me like a hawk.

I'd started having nightly dreams of running away, of leaving this life behind and fleeing with the Lost Boys to someplace my father would never find us. To someplace Barrett King would never find me.

But half the time, those dreams turned into nightmares, horrible scenarios where my father found us anyway—and when that happened, it never ended well.

I woke from those dreams in a cold sweat, panic beating against my ribs until they ached. Then I would flop back onto my bed and stare up at the ceiling, thoughts whirling around in my head.

Could I ever leave this life behind? Was that even an

option? Or would I be putting the boys I loved at risk if I even tried?

My father wasn't a man who was used to being denied anything he wanted. And with his insistence that I marry Barrett King, he had proved to me beyond any shadow of doubt that he was willing to put his own self-interests before anyone else's. Even his daughter's.

When I got home from school on the Friday after Valentine's Day, Mom caught me before I could slip upstairs to my room.

"Cordelia, I'll be sending Poppy upstairs soon to help you dress and get ready. We'll be going out to dinner with the King family this evening."

"What?" I blurted, my stomach twisting.

I hadn't spoken to Barrett once since the day I had caught him with his hand up that girl's skirt. Since the day he had proved himself to be as callous and self-serving as my father. And I had absolutely no desire to sit next to him in a fancy restaurant and pretend not to hate him. I had missed spending Valentine's day with the boys I loved, and that had been bad enough. This would just be adding insult to injury.

"You heard me," she said dismissively, turning away. "Be ready by seven-thirty sharp."

I gritted my teeth as I stared at her retreating back. Tension still bubbled between her and my father, and I was starting to think this was going to be the new normal. As hypocritical as it was, considering his reaction when I'd told

him about Barrett, my father would never forgive her for
cheating on him with Mark Jemison while he was in prison.

And of course they wouldn't divorce each other. She
needed his money, and he needed to maintain the illusion
that we were a functional family. That everything under his
roof was perfect.

It's not though. It's all falling apart.

———

POPPY CAME up to my room just as Mom had promised
she would, and spent over an hour arranging my hair into an
elaborate updo and doing my makeup. Then she helped me
into a dress that'd been picked out and left in the closet
for me.

It was a routine that was so familiar I knew every step by
heart—but it still felt utterly wrong. It felt like putting on a
costume for a role I no longer wanted to play, and I tugged
uncomfortably at the strapless dress as I stepped out of my
room.

A driver took us to the restaurant, an exclusive
establishment located on the top floor of one of the buildings
downtown. I was sure my father had chosen it to prove that
he could afford the best of the best again. My parents were
both dressed to the nines too, and everything about this
evening seemed designed to impress.

This was a calculated power play, and once again, I was
being used as a pawn by my father as he negotiated with

Sebastian King. I was sure they were still working out the details of the marriage arrangement; that was the point of this dinner, not a celebration of "young love."

As we stepped into the space, which was surrounded on all sides by floor to ceiling windows that allowed diners to overlook Baltimore below, something shifted between my parents. They stepped closer together, and instead of the tight, strained expressions they wore around each other at home, they both put on easy smiles.

Barrett and his parents had already arrived, and all three of them rose to greet us. His mother took my hands and kissed both of my cheeks, and I had to work hard not to jerk away from her touch. Sebastian's gaze flicked over me before moving to Dad, and Barrett caught my gaze and gave a smile that made my skin crawl.

"Shall we?" Sebastian gestured to the chairs around the table.

I ended up sitting between my father and Barrett, and I couldn't help but wonder if Dad had chosen a seat next to me on purpose. It felt like he was keeping a close watch on me as the adults settled into bland conversation and the waitress came by to take our order.

My stomach clenched, and I shifted uncomfortably in my chair, a flush of heat creeping up my chest. Between the way Barrett kept intentionally brushing up against me and the sidelong glances my dad kept shooting me, I felt like I was under a microscope.

Trapped.

Pinned.

Helpless.

Our food was delivered, and I tried to force down a few bites, but it turned to sawdust in my mouth. Something was building up under my skin, an agitation I couldn't shake off or tamp down.

"I'm thinking early July for the wedding," my father was saying, smiling jovially at Sebastian King. "I know it's young to be getting married by today's standards, but I see no reason to delay." He glanced at Mom with such an adoring look that even I almost believed it. "After all, we were married young. When it's right, it's right. There's no fighting it."

"Yeah, and how's that working out for you now?" I muttered, scoffing a little.

Dad stiffened beside me, his reaction immediate.

Fuck. I hadn't meant to say that out loud. I hadn't meant to speak any of my angry, bitter thoughts aloud. The words had slipped off my tongue before I could stop them.

And the entire table had heard.

Mr. and Mrs. King gazed at me with expressions that looked torn between curiosity and shock, and Barrett had narrowed his eyes. Maybe he was wondering if this was the sort of back-talk he was in for when he became my husband.

The insane, reckless urge to show him that he'd be in for that and much worse rose up inside me, and unbidden, my mouth opened again.

"But then again, I guess there's no harm in making a commitment so young, as long as you know you can always sample other flavors later," I said with a lazy shrug of my shoulders.

Almost as soon as the words were out of my mouth, a hand clamped around my arm.

"Excuse us, please."

Dad flashed a tight smile at the rest of the table as everyone's gazes flicked from him to me. Without bothering to give any further explanation or excuse, he escorted me away, keeping his grip firm on my upper arm. He pulled me toward a small nook off to one side of the restaurant, and as soon as we were out of view of everyone, he released me, straightening to his full height and glaring down at me.

"What the *fuck* are you doing, Cordelia?"

His harsh curse brought to mind the conversation where he'd promised he would no longer treat me like a child, but like an adult in all of this. That he would no longer coddle me or play nice because I was too young to understand.

He'd obviously meant it. Anger filled every line of his body, and he dipped his head, bringing it closer to my eye level.

"You don't think I know what you're trying to do? That you're trying to humiliate me in front of a man who's about to become my business partner? That you're trying to devalue the name Van Rensselaer? That's enough, Cora. I've allowed you some freedom, some leeway, hoping that if I let you have that space, you would eventually come around to accept this marriage arrangement. Instead, for every inch I've given you, you've taken a mile and thrown it back in my face."

He stepped closer to me, his lips pressing together as anger vibrated from him.

"That ends now. You are going to marry Barrett King, and until you learn to accept that and be pleasant about it, to *respect* your mother and me, the privileges that you've grown so used to are revoked." His gaze darkened, flicking toward the table before landing on me again. "This is too important to risk, Cordelia. You *will* obey me."

TEN

MY FATHER HADN'T BEEN KIDDING.

He hadn't been bluffing.

After our little conversation in the alcove at the restaurant, he had re-affixed the charming smile to his face and brought me back to the table. He and Sebastian King had come to an agreement that the wedding would take place in July, and the entire evening had continued with an air of forced joviality as I had sat silent and wooden in my chair.

And as soon as we had returned home, Dad had taken the keys to the Aston Martin.

My heart had nearly dropped into my stomach at the sight of him pocketing the keys. That car had felt like my one piece of freedom, and losing it felt like watching the walls of my prison tighten around me.

I had expected him to declare that a driver would take me to school every day, but apparently, I'd pissed him off with my backtalk more than I had realized. Because my father went one step further and pulled me from classes at Highland Park.

He called on Monday to make arrangements with the school, blaming stress and bad health, and a private tutor was hired to come teach me at home.

If he thought he was punishing me by refusing to let me attend the private academy full of the children of the elite, he was dead fucking wrong about that. I had never re-adjusted to that place, and I really didn't have any friends left inside those walls.

But what did hurt—what shredded my soul—was that I could no longer sneak out to see the Lost Boys. I wasn't allowed to leave the house for any reason, so I couldn't even take a bus across town.

I texted them as soon as I found out what my father had planned, and then deleted our entire text thread. He hadn't confiscated my phone yet, but if he did, I didn't want to give him access to everything my boys and I had sent each other.

My finger shook as I tapped the *delete* button, and my heart ached. They were just texts, hundreds of little messages sent back and forth, but they felt like keepsakes somehow. Like little pieces of the Lost Boys I had managed to carry with me all this time.

I still had their numbers, but I deleted every new text I received after reading it, keeping my phone clean of evidence in case my father decided to take my grounding one step further and confiscate my cell phone too.

The first few days of my forced isolation felt like hell. The woman Dad had hired to tutor me arrived every morning at nine o'clock sharp, and I went through several mind-numbing hours of studying with her. But that wasn't the worst part. At least during the days, I had something to keep me busy.

At night though, an acute sense of loneliness and isolation crept in.

The Lost Boys did what they could to keep my spirits up, but even through text, I could read the worry hidden behind their words. This wasn't good, and we all knew it.

By the fourth day of my father's punishment, I woke up feeling almost numb. As I stared at myself in the foggy bathroom mirror after stepping out of the shower, I realized I had to do *something* while I was locked up like this, or I really would go mad. I'd lose hope entirely, and I couldn't afford to do that.

So that evening, I went to my father's office after dinner.

He was behind his desk as usual, talking on the phone in an urgent voice. He looked up as I entered and held up a finger, and I waited until he'd wrapped up his phone call to step forward.

"Yes, Cordelia?" He set the phone down, fixing me with a wary look, as if wondering how I was going to cause him trouble this time.

"I just wanted to..." I hesitated, then forced myself to continue. "I wanted to say I'm sorry. What I did was wrong."

He lifted one brow skeptically. "Well, that's very nice of

you to say. But if you think it's going to get you out of facing
the consequences of your—"

"No, that's not it at all," I said quickly. "I'm not trying to
get out of anything. I just wanted to say I'm sorry. I was out of
sorts that night, but it won't happen again."

"I hope not, Cora." Dad's expression was stern. "I won't
tolerate it."

"I know." I bit my lip, my heart beating a little faster. "Do
you have the wedding plans on your computer? I'd just like to
see what you have so far."

A pleased look crossed his face at that, and he nodded,
gesturing me closer as he turned toward the large computer
screen that sat to one side of his desk. I moved quickly, my
gaze falling to his fingers as they flew over the keys. He had
typed out his password in front of me several times before,
but I had never paid any attention then.

Now, though, I watched each keystroke like a hawk,
repeating the sequence over and over in my head even as the
computer unlocked and my father pulled up his
correspondence with the wedding planner my parents had
hired. If I had been any other daughter and he'd been any
other father, maybe I would've been touched that he was so
deeply involved in the wedding planning process.

But I wasn't.

He wasn't.

And I knew just what this was about.

He wanted control over the entire event, just like he
wanted control over everything else in his life.

I feigned interest as he showed me the planned venue, even though my entire body tensed at the thought of walking down the aisle in the huge, ornate church to stand next to a boy I despised. Careful to keep my inner thoughts off my face, I turned to my Dad and dipped my head.

"Thank you. I just... I just wanted to know."

"That's good." He smiled. "I knew you would come around to this. I'm happy to see you finally are."

I'm not! I wanted to scream. *I never fucking will.*

But I kept my lips shut and slipped from the room.

———

THE NEXT DAY, as soon as my tutor left at three o'clock, I made a beeline toward my father's office. He was working from his office downtown today, and Mom was out doing who knew what.

I slipped into the large, opulent room and glanced over my shoulder as I slid into the chair behind the desk. I had been repeating the password to myself all morning, focusing on that combination of letters and numbers more than any of my actual schoolwork, and I tapped it out carefully on the keyboard.

Relief and gratitude rushed through me when the computer unlocked, the screen shifting to show several icons and file folders. Not sure how much time I would have before Dad or Mom got back home, I moved quickly, opening up the web browser before double-clicking on several files. I wasn't quite sure what I was looking for, but I hoped I would recognize it when I saw it.

I'd spent months trying to guess whether my father was really guilty of the crimes he'd been accused of or not, and although he'd been released in the end, I needed to know for myself just what exactly he *had* done.

He may not have done what he was arrested for, but that didn't automatically make him a good person. He had claimed he wanted to turn over a new leaf when he got out of prison, but I no longer believed that. And I wanted to know what kinds of things he had willingly done in the pursuit of more power and prestige.

"Come on, where are you? Show me something. *Anything*," I muttered, clicking open his email.

The cops had been through all of his stuff, and in the end, the only evidence of actual illegal activity turned out to have been planted. But still, I was sure my father had skirted as close to the line as he thought he could get away with, and I wanted to know the truth.

I spent close to an hour poring over his files and emails, and then my fingers hesitated over the keyboard. I held my breath, peering closer at the screen at a name I recognized.

Abraham Shaw.

That was the name I had heard Flint mention all those weeks ago. Abraham had been a colleague of my father's, and I was pretty sure they had worked closely together for several years.

My heart beat faster as I scanned through several email

exchanges between the two of them, chewing on my lower lip.

Fuck. Dad didn't break the law. Abraham did.

It wasn't spelled out explicitly, but as I read email after email, I became more and more certain that I was right. My father had leveraged his partnership with Abraham to make sure that every illegal action they had taken was traceable only to Mr. Shaw. That would've left Dad free to deny any knowledge or involvement if Abraham ever went down—except that Dad had ended up being framed instead.

Abraham must've worked with Luke Carmine to set my father up, using his inside knowledge of the crimes they'd committed to make a compelling case against Dad.

But the truth was, *both* men were guilty.

Anger burned in my veins, and I decided to follow the rabbit down the hole as far as I could go.

The first thing I needed to do was dig up more information on the history between my dad and his old business associate, so I searched all of his files for the name *Abraham Shaw*. A lot of what I found was boring and indecipherable, contracts and discussions of acquisitions that made no sense to me. But when I pulled up file marked "Untitled," I found something much different.

It was the record of a payment from my father... to Luke Carmine.

I felt like I had cotton in my lungs. It was almost impossible to draw a full breath, but I forced myself to keep reading.

Holy fuck. That's exactly what it is.

Abraham Shaw had paid Luke Carmine to destroy my father's life, but he wasn't the only one who'd had that idea. If I was reading this right, my dad had tried to screw over Abraham Shaw, to recruit Luke to take his old business partner down several weeks before my father's own arrest. But Abraham must've offered more money or a better deal, because he'd somehow gotten Luke on his side instead.

I blinked, staring at the screen as I tried to process this strange turn of events. No wonder my father had been so certain he'd been set up—he had been in the process of trying to set his once-friend up when he'd been arrested.

Does he know that Luke is the one who arranged the frame job that landed him in prison? That he was double-crossed?

As I gazed blankly at the screen, a door slammed in the distance.

My body tensed as my head whipped up, and I quickly closed up the apps on my dad's desktop, put the computer back to sleep, and bolted from the room. I ran up the stairs on tiptoes, my bare feet silent on the smooth marble, and when I reached my room, I closed the door and leaned against it, sliding down until my ass hit the floor.

Everything he's told me is a lie.

My father had pretended he was an honest-dealing businessman who'd been wrongly accused, set up when he was totally innocent.

But he wasn't innocent.

He was as guilty as Abraham. Maybe even more so.

I wasn't sure why that even surprised me anymore. But it did. Despite everything that'd happened over the past several months, there was a part of me that had still clung to hope that *some* parts of my life hadn't been based on lies.

But as I looked around at the lavish surroundings of my large room, I felt more like a stranger in this place than I ever had before.

It wasn't just that I didn't belong here now.

I had never belonged here.

ELEVEN

I TOLD Poppy I wasn't feeling well when she came to fetch me for dinner, and although I expected one of my parents to come and drag me downstairs, neither of them knocked on my door.

My stomach kept tying itself into tighter and tighter knots as my thoughts spun around in my head. I couldn't quite figure out why it bothered me so much that my father had broken the law. After all, the Lost Boys broke the law all the time. They worked for a man and for an organization that thrived on illegal activity.

So what was the difference?

Honor, a little voice in the back of my head whispered.

The Lost Boys had it. Even Nathaniel Ward had it.

They all existed on the wrong side of the law, but they still lived their lives according to their principles. Their own moral code.

The Lost Boys could be threatening and dangerous, but they used their power at Slateview High to keep the peace —something not even the school admins or teachers could do.

Nathaniel was ruthless in his operation, but even he had lines in the sand he wouldn't cross.

My father, though?

I kept waiting for him to reveal a better side of himself, but instead, he showed me over and over again the lengths he would go to for his own benefit.

It made me sick to think about how much of the wealth and privilege I'd grown up with had probably been acquired by someone else's downfall. That seemed to be my father's usual method of operation.

The dinner hour came and went, and even though I'd planned to sneak down for food later in the evening, I had completely lost my appetite. At a little after nine, I threw on a soft nightgown and brushed my teeth, then crawled into bed, eager for sleep to claim me.

It did, and quickly.

My whirling thoughts slowed as the pain in my chest settled into a dull, throbbing ache, and my eyelids drifted closed.

When they flew open several hours later, I wasn't sure what had woken me until I heard the sound of my phone ringing again. I rolled toward the nightstand and snatched it up, blinking blearily at the screen. The time read 12:02, and the caller ID read *Bishop*.

A little jolt of adrenaline ran through me as happiness that he was calling mixed with worry.

Why he is calling so late? Did something happen?

I swiped to answer quickly, bringing the phone to my ear. My parents were in an entirely different wing of the house, so I knew they wouldn't hear me, but I kept my voice low anyway.

"Bishop? Is everything okay? What's going on?"

"Happy birthday, Coralee."

His smooth drawl cut through my fear like a knife, and I blinked into the darkness. "What?"

"Well, it's your birthday today, isn't it?"

"Y-yes. Just for the past few minutes, yeah."

"What kind of boyfriends would we be if we didn't call to wish you a happy birthday?"

Something so sweet I could hardly bear it spread through my chest, and I closed my eyes, dragging in a deep breath.

"We miss you, Cora," Misael said softly, and I realized Bish must've put me on speaker phone.

"So fucking much," Kace added, and the strain in his voice told me more than his words ever could.

They missed me the same way I missed them. With a deep, aching hunger, a need that would never be satisfied by anything else.

"I miss you guys too," I whispered, not even trying to hide the naked emotion in my voice.

I had been dreading my eighteenth birthday. In my mind, all it did was bring me one step closer to becoming a married woman, and I'd had no desire to celebrate it. But the fact that the Lost Boys had remembered, that they'd called just a few minutes after midnight because they couldn't even wait until tomorrow to wish me a happy birthday—it made a smile curve my lips even as tears pricked my eyes.

They cared for me.

And they didn't just tell me that, like my father and mother did. Like so many of my friends did.

They showed me. Over and over, in big ways and little ones, they showed me how much they cared.

"I wish you were here."

"We wish we were too, Princess," Misael said quietly. "But we didn't want to risk it again after last time. We don't want to get you in more trouble. If you want us to though, we'll be over in—"

"No!" I almost sat up, then settled back down, still clutching the phone to my ear. "No. Don't. I don't want to risk you getting caught. I just... I just wish I could see you, is all."

My voice broke on the words, and I could hear each of them react with a low noise. I could imagine them all sitting on Bishop's couch as he held the phone out, could picture them all leaning toward it slightly as if that might somehow bring them closer to me.

For a moment, there was silence on the line. It felt heavy, full of all the things none of us were saying. All of our fears, our worries. Our pain at being separated.

Finally, Bishop spoke. "What would you do if we were there right now?"

There was a teasing growl in his words, and I knew he was trying to distract me from my heartache. It didn't quite work, but I loved that he was trying. And despite the pain that still bounced around in my chest, I smiled slightly as I considered my answer.

"I would kiss you. I'd kiss each of you, over and over and over. Until I could taste all of you on my tongue. On my lips."

A soft groan came through the line, and I was pretty sure it came from Kace. An answering ripple of heat moved through my lower belly, and I squirmed under the soft blankets.

"What would *you* do if you were here?" I whispered.

"How 'bout this, Coralee?" Misael said. There was something in his voice that made my breath come faster. "We'll tell you what we'd do, if you promise to do it."

"What do you mean?"

The butterflies flapping in my stomach insisted they already knew exactly what he meant, but I wanted to hear him say it. An ache was building inside me, making my core feel swollen and needy. It'd been too long since I'd seen these boys who owned three pieces of my soul. Too long since I'd touched them.

"Since we can't be there, you'll have to do it for us." Misael's tone was low and teasing, and I could picture the mischievous glint in his dark eyes. "So if I say I'd run my hands over your milky skin, that I'd squeeze your tits and play with your nipples till you were moaning and writhing..."

My breath caught in my throat, and a gush of wetness dampened my panties.

"Then I would do it," I whispered, one hand gripping the phone tighter while the other began to roam my own body, pushing the fabric of my nightgown out of the way as my fingertips teased my nipple.

"Yeah." His voice was strangled, and I swore I could hear heavier breathing from the other two boys. "Do it for me, Coralee. Let me hear you moan."

His words seemed to travel straight to my clit, and just as he had commanded, I writhed restlessly, my hand massaging my breast with a harder touch as I pinched and pulled my nipple. When I switched to the other one, it was already peaked and sensitive, and I let out a low groan as my clit throbbed.

"Fuck, yes. Like that."

Kace's voice was hard and rough, and I moaned again at the sound of it. Everything about these boys turned me on, and if all I could have right now was their voices, their grunts and moans, I would take it.

"Kace," I murmured, still tugging hard on my nipples, making jagged bolts of sensation tear through me. "I want your cock in my mouth. I want to suck you and lick you until you can't take it anymore."

I had never understood why his dirty talk always turned me on so much, making my whole body electric with need even as it made me blush. I still didn't quite understand it, but my own filthy words were having the same effect on me, as each word brought with it a vivid image, a remembered sensation.

"I like when you grab my hair while I'm sucking you," I said. My hand left my breasts, trailing down over my stomach before delving beneath the waistband of my panties. "I like when you use me like that."

"Fucking hell, Princess."

He sounded like he might be dying. Like my words might be killing him.

I grinned, biting my lower lip. I liked having this kind of power over him—liked being able to drive him crazy like this. But I didn't want him to die. I didn't want to torture him.

My hand moved down farther between my legs, brushing over my clit before delving into my wet core, and my entire body shuddered.

"I'm touching myself," I murmured. "You guys touch yourselves too. Imagine it's me. My hand. My mouth. My... pussy. My ass."

I stumbled over the words a little, but any embarrassment or awkwardness I might've felt was fading quickly as sensations flooded me. For the first time in days, I felt *right*. I felt happy and whole.

"Fuck," Bishop bit out, and I could picture his cock straining against his pants.

"Uh, Princess, normally when we all take out our dicks around each other, it's 'cause you're here. You're in the middle of all of us," Misael commented, humor in his voice. But I could hear the need there too.

They might never have done something like this before, but I was almost sure they would tonight. Because I had asked. Because they never liked to deny me anything. And because they needed this just as much as I did.

"I am there," I said softly, bringing my arousal-slicked fingers up to rub at my clit, teasing myself with light touches at first. "I'm right there with you. I want you all so fucking bad."

"Fucking Christ."

Kace's words burst out of him, and a second later, I heard the unmistakable sound of a zipper, and the rustling of clothing.

My heart rate spiked, my clit throbbing harder and harder as my fingers worked faster.

"Are you touching yourself, Kace?" I gasped.

"Yes," he gritted out, his voice clipped. "Fuckin' my fist. Wish it was your tight little pussy."

My whole body jerked at the sound of his words. I was on the verge of coming already, but I didn't slow my fingers. I didn't want to hold it off. I would come for these boys. Then I would come again, and again, and again.

"I don't," I rasped, arching my back, rubbing my sensitive nipples against the blankets. "I want you in my ass. Just like you promised. It'll be tight, Kace. I know it'll be so tight. But I know you'll take care of me. You'll make it feel good."

The breathing coming through the line was heavier now,

three distinct patterns of breath. I could hear other noises too, more wet sounds of flesh on flesh, that made me certain the other boys were touching themselves too.

"I'll always take care of you, Princess," Kace muttered, a dark promise in his voice that made my toes curl and my hips buck off the mattress.

"Oh, God," I whispered brokenly. "Gonna come. Gonna—"

My core and my ass both clenched rhythmically as an orgasm plowed into me, and I had never felt more empty in my life.

"Shit, that's the best sound in the world." Bishop's voice was thick and heavy with desire. "Do it again for us. Don't stop."

I didn't. My clit was still throbbing with aftershocks, but my fingers kept moving, circling around it as I brought myself back toward the edge again.

"Bishop," I choked out. "I want you inside me at the same time. I want you both inside me. I want you to fill me up with your cum."

"Jesus."

Low grunts punctuated that word, and I could tell from the sounds reaching my ears that they were all getting closer too. It'd been too long for all of us.

"I'd like that, Princess," Bishop murmured. "I'd grab your hips and hold you steady so we could both fuck you hard. Could you take it? Could you take us both?"

"Uh-huh." I was whimpering, losing the ability to speak

in full sentences as the need inside me built again. "Misael too. I want all of you. Please... please, oh fuck, please."

Before the words were all the way out of my mouth, I came again, my whole body shuddering as euphoria flooded my veins.

My panties were soaked through, wetness dripping from my core and smearing my thighs, and the frantic movement of my fingers drew the orgasm out into one long wave of pleasure, making my breath hitch as if I'd had the wind knocked out of me.

But I still didn't stop. My clit was pulsing, almost painfully sensitive, but I kept touching myself. I wasn't done yet. My boys hadn't come yet. And I was still hungry for more.

I rolled over onto my side, pinning the phone between the pillow and my head so I could free up my other hand. My fingertips brushed across my skin, lighting up my nerve endings as my thighs squeezed together, trapping my hand between them as I rode my own touch with hungry undulations of my hips.

"I want to hear you come," I rasped. "I want to picture it. I want to feel it."

"Fuck, Cora." Kace swore under his breath, and I had a feeling he was on the verge of driving over and breaking into my parents' house no matter how dangerous it was.

"Come for me, Kace," I whispered, my heart thudding against my ribs. "Imagine it's my mouth. My tongue. Imagine how deep you'd go. You'd make me cry. And I'd love it."

A choked grunt came through the line, and then the sound of deep, ragged breathing.

"Jesus fuckin' Christ, Princess," Bishop grated. "Who taught you to talk so dirty?"

"You did." I bit my lip, sliding two fingers inside myself. The stretch was nowhere near as satisfying as one of their cocks, but I let my imagination take over, grinding the heel of my hand against my clit. "You taught me to be dirty. You showed me how much I like it."

Misael gave a low, animalistic grunt that I recognized as his release, and a second later, Bishop let loose a stream of curses. I fucked myself hard and fast with my fingers, and when the fourth orgasm hit me like a speeding car, my body jerked so hard the phone slipped away from my ear.

For a second, I couldn't move. Could barely think.

But I missed the sounds of the boys breathing; I needed that connection with them. After groping around on the bed near my head, I located my cell phone and held it to my ear, grinning when I heard the boys again. They were all breathing hard, and Bishop finally let out a choppy laugh.

"Well, fuck. Jerking off on a couch next to my two best friends. It's not the weirdest Friday night I've ever had, but it's close."

"Fuckin' worth it," Misael groaned, sounding so happy and satisfied that it made my heart swell.

It had never been a question that the three boys would share me. I had developed feelings for all of them at the same time, and they were all such a tight-knit unit that I didn't think any of them had questioned it either. But this was a first for all of us, and I loved that they trusted each other enough—and cared about me enough—to do it.

"Yeah." Kace's voice was a bit softer than usual, a bit sweeter. "But I still miss you, Princess."

"A-fuckin'-men," Misael agreed.

"I miss you guys too."

My body was drifting toward sleep again after the intensity of the sensations that'd torn through me. But I wasn't ready to let go yet. I wasn't ready to say goodbye.

"Thank you," I whispered sleepily, my eyes drifting closed. "For calling. For everything."

"Always, Princess."

We hung up a moment later, but I kept the phone cradled in my grip, and I fell asleep that way, comforted by the knowledge that I wasn't alone.

TWELVE

ANOTHER TWO WEEKS passed before my father decided I'd been sufficiently punished for my outburst at the restaurant. I had half-expected him to keep me on lockdown for the remainder of the semester, but of course, that didn't fit with the illusion of a perfect family with a perfect life he was trying so hard to maintain.

It probably helped that I had decided to play along with his game, and had made myself the picture of contrition every time I was in his presence. I snuck into his home office two more times while he was out of the house, printing off a few things and keeping them hidden under my mattress.

I wasn't exactly sure why I did it, or what I planned to do with the things I'd printed. He'd been careful to keep his tracks covered, so nothing on his computer or his inbox was directly incriminating. I wasn't sure anything I'd found would be solid enough to become real blackmail material, even if I was brave enough to attempt to blackmail my own father.

My gut twisted every time I thought about possibilities like that, making me feel nauseated and shaky. It was terrifying to even think of imploding my family like that, but it was even more terrifying to consider what my dad might do if backed into a corner. He'd shown me quite clearly that he didn't like to lose, and that he would go to extreme lengths to get what he wanted.

But he liked to pretend he was reasonable and magnanimous, so in the face of my apparent penitence, he agreed to let me go back to school. He even gave me back the Aston Martin, although that too was probably more for appearances than anything else. He couldn't stand the idea of his daughter not keeping up with the other children of the elite.

My three week absence had been noticed by everyone at school, and in my absence, the contingent of people who hated me seemed to have grown in both strength and numbers. It almost felt like more of a punishment to have to walk the halls of Highland Park Academy than to listen to Katherine quiz me on the contents of my textbooks.

By the middle of my first days back, I could already feel my patience straining at the seams. In my last class of the day, I snuck my phone out of my bag and pulled up a new text message.

ME: *I have to get out of here for a little while. Can I see you guys?*

BISHOP: *We're close by. We'll come pick you up at 3.*

I knew they worried about me driving my fancy-ass car into the neighborhood I'd lived in with Mom for a few months, so I didn't put up a fight.

ME: *Okay. I'll be out front.*

Then I shot a text to Mom telling her that I had to stay late at school for a prom committee meeting. I knew Dad had demanded that she not let me go places outside of school, but with the tension still so thick between them, I was pretty sure she wasn't about to go tell on me. They were hardly a united force when it came to parenting.

As soon as the class ended, I scooped up my bag and bolted for the door, making my way through the throngs of people in the hallways until I reached the front of the school and jogged down the steps.

Unfortunately, I was so excited to get outside that I didn't see Marissa until she stepped in front of me as I hurried down the sidewalk. She'd been president of the *We Hate Cora Club* ever since I'd punched her in the face, and her open sneer told me her feelings toward me hadn't changed one bit.

"Watch where the fuck you're going, you slut!" she hissed, her lips curling back in an expression that closely resembled a snarl.

Before I could respond, a deep voice from behind me made pleasant goose bumps rise along my skin.

"No, *you* watch where the fuck you're going."

Bishop, Kace, and Misael stepped up beside me, moving

like a rolling wave toward the redheaded girl in front of me. They stopped when they reached her, all three of them towering over her.

"Watch who the fuck you're talkin' to while you're at it," Misael added. "There ain't shit you have to say to Cora that she wants to hear, get me?"

Marissa blinked. She was partially obscured from view by the three boys between us, but I could see several expressions flit over her face as she tried to come up with a response.

I could see her reaching for entitlement and superiority, but she seemed to be having a hard time latching onto them in the face of the sheer intimidating presence of these three boys. Finally, she shot a glance at me, then scoffed derisively and walked away—a little bit faster than she needed to.

Suppressing a grin at the fear she couldn't quite hide, I poked Kace in the back. "You guys didn't have to do that. I have her handled."

He looked over his shoulder at me, his moss-green eyes blazing with fierce pride. "Oh, we know that, Princess. Just figured we'd save your right hook for another day."

The other boys both laughed, and he draped an arm around my shoulder as they led me toward their car. We got in quickly, and as soon as we pulled away from the school, I looked around at all of them.

"So, where are going?"

"One guess." Misael grinned.

I rolled my eyes. "Nathaniel's?"

"Got it on the first try."

I laughed. The truth was, I didn't mind going to Nathaniel Ward's place. It was certainly more comfortable than going back to my own house, where tension choked the air constantly. For such a massive place, my parents' house somehow managed to feel incredibly claustrophobic.

And honestly, I would've gone anywhere as long as it meant I got to be with the Lost Boys. It had been way too long since I'd seen them, and my body buzzed with joyful energy just being in the same space as the three of them.

When we arrived at Nathaniel's place thirty minutes later, the butler didn't bring us up to the office as usual. Instead, he escorted us deeper into the house on the first floor, stopping in a large sitting room. Nathaniel was sitting in a chair near an ornate fireplace, and Josephine perched on one arm of the chair.

His arm was draped possessively around her waist, and she had her head bowed, speaking low into his ear. Whatever she said made him smile, and it wasn't an expression I'd ever seen him wear before. It made him look almost boyish.

The butler nodded to us and slipped out, and I wished he would've walked with a heavier step or announced our presence or something—although I was sure the fact that he didn't was due to the fact that the Lost Boys had become regular fixtures around here. But when Josephine and Nathaniel got wrapped up in the bubble of each other, it was hard not to feel like an intruder on a private moment.

Is that what I'm like with my boys?

Probably. When I was with them, the rest of the world

often seemed to fade away, becoming nothing more than a dull blur in the background. I didn't notice or care if we drew stares. None of that mattered.

Bishop stepped forward, and as he did, the couple looked up at us. Josephine's gaze landed on me, and she smiled brightly. Nathaniel nodded approvingly at the men.

"Good. I'm glad you're here. Claudio Vega will be coming for dinner this evening, and he requested that you three be there." His gaze shifted to me. "You as well, Ms. Van Rensselaer, if you'd like."

"Um, sure."

I grinned. I liked being included in the Lost Boys' lives, and I could have dinner and still not get home too late. Maybe I was a little stir-crazy from having been locked up for three weeks, but it felt fucking amazing to be out of my parents' house.

"You'll need something to wear." Josephine rose from the arm of the chair in a graceful movement. "We're close to the same size. Come with me. I'll find something for you."

I cast a glance at my three boys, and they all nodded. It wasn't that I distrusted Josephine, although her husband still intimidated the hell out of me. But this was the boys' world, and I trusted their judgement on these things. They all seemed comfortable with the idea of me staying, probably because our first meeting with Claudio had gone well.

"Sure," I said, turning back to Josephine. "Thanks."

"Of course."

She headed for the door, gesturing for me to follow her.

Then she led me up the stairs, turning in the opposite direction from Nathaniel's office. When she stepped inside what I was pretty sure was their bedroom, I hesitated, chewing my lip.

"It's alright. I won't bite."

She chuckled, and I shook my head, laughing at myself. "Right. Sorry."

"There's nothing to be sorry for." She smiled at me, then crossed to her closet and began rifling through it. She shot a look over her shoulder at me. "How are things at home? The boys missed you these past few weeks."

My heart thudded unevenly against my ribs. If Josephine had noticed my absence in their lives and observed that the boys missed me, it must've been pretty fucking obvious. The time apart had been torture for me, and I hated to think of them in pain too.

"It's... okay." The word sounded like the lie it was. "I don't know. I'm not sure what to do."

Sympathy and concern crossed Josephine's face. "I'm sorry, Cora."

She pulled a dress from the closet and crossed back to me. It was beautiful, elegant and well-made, but different than any of the dresses that hung in my own closet. It was more striking. More daring.

Just like Josephine herself.

She held up the gown in front of me and nodded in satisfaction. "Perfect. You can change in there."

She directed me to the en suite bathroom, and I quickly

pulled off my skirt, top, and blazer, then slipped into the dress. It fit surprisingly well, and I turned from side-to-side, gazing at my reflection in the mirror.

I looked like me, but... different. The dress was black, with a light sheen to the fabric and detailing in gold thread that bumped it up from just a classic black cocktail dress to something else entirely. It hugged the curves of my body, subtly showing off the soft dips and swells, and the flashes of gold as I moved highlighted my blonde hair.

It was stunning.

And it made me look older, somehow. More self-possessed. I liked it.

When I stepped out of the bathroom, Josephine's gaze landed on me, and she smiled, the corners of her eyes crinkling slightly. There was something almost like pride in her gaze, and it made an unexpected swell of emotion rise in me. It was a look like a mother might give her child, although I couldn't remember the last time my own mother had looked at me like that.

It occurred to me for the first time that Josephine and Nathaniel didn't have children. Or at least, none that I was aware of. Was that by choice or by circumstances outside their control?

I wasn't about to pry by asking, so I just smiled shyly and spun in a circle, letting Josephine see her handiwork. "What do you think?"

"I think it's perfect." She beamed at me. "I think I may

just have to give you that dress, since it's obviously so much better suited to you than to me."

"Oh, no."

I waved a hand, trying to brush her off, and she chuckled. She pulled a pair of shoes from her closet and brought them over to me, and when I slipped them on, it brought us to nearly the same height.

She gave me another once-over before nodding approvingly. Then she surprised the hell out of me by wrapping her arms around my shoulders in a gentle hug.

"I wish I could give you more help or better advice, Cora. I've been somewhere very close to where you are now, and I know how terrifying and confusing it is. But remember this: you're not alone."

THIRTEEN

JOSEPHINE SENT me back downstairs while she picked out her own outfit for the evening. It felt strange to walk through the house unaccompanied by the butler or even my own boys. It was a level of trust and comfortability I had never expected to achieve with the Wards, and I had to remind myself to keep my guard up, at least a little.

When I found the stairs that led back to the main floor, I stepped down them slowly, listening for the sound of voices. I could hear the boys and Nathaniel in the sitting room, talking amiably amongst themselves, but the moment I stepped inside the room, the conversation died out.

Bishop, Misael, and Kace all rose to their feet, the movement seeming almost unconscious. As if they'd been pulled by some magnetic force, they stepped toward me, their gazes raking over my body with such hunger and possessiveness that I felt my cheeks warm.

"You look..." Misael shook his head, seeming at a loss for words. "Damn, Coralee."

Nathaniel's focus shifted from the boys to me and back again, and although there wasn't the same heat in his eyes as I saw in theirs, he wore an expression of approval.

"Join us, Cora. Please."

He gestured to the couch near the fireplace, and the three boys escorted me back to it, their small touches traveling through my body like liquid lightning. Josephine joined us a little while later, and the six of us fell into a surprisingly relaxed conversation as we waited for Claudio and his people to arrive.

By the time the butler ushered Claudio inside, I had almost completely forgotten that the people I was spending time with were hardened criminals. Nathanial's sheer power and charisma still terrified me a little, but he had a surprisingly wicked sense of humor, sharp and dry.

As soon as Claudio arrived, a subtle shift seemed to take place in the atmosphere, and the true purpose of this dinner clarified in my mind once again. This wasn't just a small dinner party. It was a negotiation between two criminal factions.

We were ushered into the dining room, and I tried to keep my glances subtle as I took in Claudio and his men. He'd brought a few of his own people, and although their postures were relaxed, I could feel how alert they were. They were bodyguards of a sort, meant to protect their leader as he walked into what could become enemy territory if the negotiations went south.

Claudio's ease was less obviously an act, although there was a sort of intense energy that radiated from him as we all sat down.

The first course was served, and the men launched into a discussion of people and topics I knew nothing about. So I didn't add much to the conversation, instead just observing and trying to guess how things were going based on the body language of the people around the table. I thought it was going well, and that assumption was confirmed when I caught Josephine's gaze and she nodded slightly.

Good.

I didn't understand the maneuverings of the Baltimore underground, but if this went well for Nathaniel, it would reflect well on my boys. And I wanted that. I wanted to see them succeed.

Our dishes were cleared before the second course was brought out, and as I glanced around the table once more, I hesitated. Claudio Vega was wearing a relaxed smile, but the intense energy that I'd sensed from him before had only increased.

My stomach tightened.

Fuck. Was this about to go bad? Had he come here not to negotiate, but to attack? He would be foolish to try anything in Nathaniel's own house—he had to know there were other men stationed around the mansion, that this place was well protected.

But if he wasn't planning something, why did Claudio seem so tense? Why did his gaze keep darting around?

A new realization struck me, and my heart pounded harder in my chest.

His gaze wasn't moving around randomly. It kept flicking in the same direction.

Toward Misael.

The boy with dark hair and caramel skin was sitting on the same side of the table as me, with Bishop between us. He seemed to have noticed Claudio's attention too, and I could tell he was on edge, ready to fight if need be.

The food I'd eaten, delicious as it was, turned into a lump of cement in my belly. I clutched my fork and knife tighter, as if I might use them in self-defense.

Should I say something? What should I say?

I didn't know all the dynamics at play here, and I was terrified that opening my mouth would only make the tension I could feel bubbling in the air snap. But before I could decide whether to open my mouth, Claudio spoke.

The conversation around the table had lulled, and in the moment of quiet, the tattooed man turned toward Misael, staring at him openly for the first time all night.

"Are you from Baltimore?"

The question surprised me, and it must've surprised Misael too, because he answered automatically. "Yes."

"Born here?"

Misael's brows drew together. "Yes."

I could see Nathaniel leaning forward a little. This line of questioning had surprised him too, and he obviously didn't like seeing one of his own people interrogated by an outsider. He opened his mouth, but before he could put a stop to things, Claudio spoke again.

"Was your mother Maria Hernandez?"

Misael's eyes flew wide. Everyone at the table turned to look at him, and I didn't even need to hear his answer to know what it would be.

Yes.

"How do you know her name?" he asked quietly, instead of replying to Claudio's question.

Claudio's face had paled slightly, and he seemed frozen in place for a long moment, as if stunned by the answer. Silence reigned over the table as everyone exchanged glances. Even Claudio's own men seemed unsure what their boss was after. They clearly hadn't expected any of this either.

After several heartbeats, Claudio shook his head.

"I... knew your mother."

My gaze swung back to Misael. Everything else seemed to have been forgotten for the moment. Whatever alliance Claudio had come here to discuss was hardly more than a distant memory now.

Because the way he spoke—the way he hesitated over the words—made me certain he had known Misael's mother as much more than a passing acquaintance.

My jaw fell open slightly as I stared at Misael, whose face was a mask of shock. *Holy fuck.* No wonder Claudio had agreed to this dinner. No wonder he had requested the Lost

Boys be present for it. Ever since the first day we'd met him at the club he owned, he must've been wanting to ask Misael these questions.

Maybe he'd known Misael would never agree to meet with him on his own. So he had agreed to come to Nathaniel's house, had decided to do this in front of everyone.

"How?"

Misael's voice was barely more than a rasp. He looked like he had turned to stone, his body was held so stiff and still.

For the first time since he'd started down this path, Claudio glanced toward Nathaniel, probably wondering if he would be allowed to continue. Nathaniel gave a minute nod, but his eyes were narrowed, his expression wary.

Claudio turned back to Misael, speaking quickly, as if he was worried he would be cut off before he was allowed to get everything out.

"When I was younger, not much older than you are now, I started working for a man named Jackson Mohan. He's since died, but he was my introduction to this world." He drew in a deep breath, keeping his gaze focused on Misael. "A few years after that, I met Maria. She wasn't like anyone I'd ever met before, and I... I fell in love with her. She loved me too."

Misael's face was still like stone. He was normally the most expressive of the Lost Boys, but at the moment, I couldn't read his thoughts at all. My own thoughts were a jumble as Claudio continued.

"We were together, your mother and I. It was the happiest I'd ever been. But I was involved in some bad shit by that point. Jackson Mahon was a dangerous man with dangerous enemies, and—" A muscle in his jaw ticked. "Your mother was almost killed because of me. She was my weak spot, my vulnerability, and people who wanted to get to me tried to do it through her. I saved her, but I couldn't let anything like that happen ever again."

My lungs burned, and I realized with a start that I had stopped breathing as I listened to him speak. No one made a sound as he paused to organize his thoughts.

"I was determined to keep Maria safe. So I left." Claudio spoke simply, but I could hear the pain buried in his voice. "If she was no longer a part of my life, no one would have any reason to hurt her. I kept my distance from her for years, and in that time, Jackson Mahon died. With his enemies off my back, I began working for myself. My life stabilized. My power and resources grew. And all that time, I never stopped thinking of Maria. I went back for her, nearly seven years after I left her behind." His lips pressed together, and his hands clenched into fists. "But she was dead."

Misael nodded. It was the first movement I'd seen him make since Claudio had begun his story. "She died when I was six."

"I didn't know." Claudio sounded pained. "When I found out she was dead, it nearly killed me too. I wish I had stayed with her, no matter the risk. I wish I had been by her side to fight for her and protect her. To care for her. The greatest regret of my life was leaving her behind."

Then he shook his head, his dark irises churning.

"Or at least it was. Until I realized I also left behind a son."

FOURTEEN

THE SILENCE that fell was so complete that it was like someone had switched off the volume on the world.

Misael stared at Claudio with unblinking eyes, his nostrils flaring as he breathed hard. Then, without warning, he shoved back his chair so violently it almost tipped over. Turning on his heel, he stalked from the room.

My heart was beating so hard and fast it felt like it was about to trip over itself. I couldn't tell quite what Misael was feeling, so I didn't know quite what *I* was feeling. All I knew was that I wanted to be there for him, to help him in any way I could.

I shot a glance at Claudio, who was staring after Misael with a pained look on his face. Then I shifted my gaze to Nathaniel, asking permission just like Claudio had. We were all still under Nathaniel's roof, after all, and I'd been a part of this world long enough to know that his word was law here.

He nodded slightly, giving me permission to leave the table, and as soon as I got the go-ahead, I stood up almost as fast as Misael had. I brushed my fingertips over Kace and Bishop's shoulders as I turned to leave. I could feel the tension in their bodies even through that small touch, and I had a feeling they wanted to kick the shit out of Claudio right now. I kind of wanted to punch him too, honestly.

Neither of the boys had stood when I did, so I left them to deal with Claudio while I headed out of the room in search of Misael. I was sure he didn't want all of us coming after him right now anyway. Truth be told, I wasn't even sure he would speak to me. But I was sure as hell gonna try.

I wandered the first floor of the house for a few minutes, searching for Misael. I finally found him in a long hallway leading toward the back of the house. He was sitting on the floor, his elbows braced on his knees and his back against the wall, head down and hair falling over his eyes.

Keeping my footsteps light, as if I was afraid he would run, I approached slowly and sank down beside him. He didn't look up, but I could feel the shift in his body as he registered my presence.

I didn't want to push him too hard, but I couldn't help myself—the need to be close to him was overwhelming. I scooted closer, until our arms were pressed together, and the heat from his body soothed me, even though I was supposed to be the one offering comfort to him.

We sat in silence for a few moments, then I murmured, "I'm sorry, Misael. This is so much to take in. Are you okay?"

He let out a low noise that was part laugh, part grunt. "I don't fuckin' know. I don't know that man, Coralee. I've only met him twice in my life."

"I know."

"My mom always told me my father was a fuckin' asshole."

My stomach clenched, and I leaned my head over to rest it on Misael's shoulder. I could feel the heavy thud of his heart as it reverberated through his whole chest.

"Maybe she thought he was. Maybe she didn't know *why* he did what he did."

"Yeah. Well, how could she when he just up and left?"

"She couldn't." My chest ached, and I breathed in the sweet scent of cloves, wishing I could steal his pain away. I would take it all into myself so he didn't have to feel it if I could.

"That's not..." He trailed off, then shook his head. "That's not what gets to me the most though. Not what fucks with my head the most."

"What is, then?"

"The whole time he was talkin', I couldn't stop thinking— that's me. That's *us*. Me and you and Kace and Bish. He said he was about our age when he started workin' for that Jackson dude. Then he met my mom and fell in love. And then people tried to fuckin' kill her."

Misael finally lifted his head, craning his neck to meet my gaze. I could see dozens of emotions swirling behind his dark brown irises, and the tortured look on his face broke my heart.

"Coralee, what if that happens to you? What if we're putting you in danger just by havin' you in our lives? Nathaniel already sent you with us to meet with Claudio. You're too deep already. What if some fucker comes after you because of us? I couldn't fuckin' live with myself if that happened."

Raw fear flooded me, coating my insides with acid. But it wasn't fear of what might happen to me if someone came after me because of my association with the Lost Boys.

It was fear of what would happen if they did what Claudio had done.

If they left me.

"Misael, *no.*" My voice was harsh and raspy as I sat up on my knees, turning sideways to face him. "No! Don't even think about that. I don't fucking care. I don't care what being in this world of yours means. If it means more danger or risk, I can live with that."

My breath felt like it was trapped in my lungs, and panic like I'd never known flooded me. For a split second, I saw a future without the Lost Boys. A future where I married Barrett and lived in a big, cold house, cut off from everything that made me *feel.*

Cut off from everything I loved.

"I love you, Misael," I blurted. "I love you so fucking much, and I don't *care* if that puts me at risk." I reached out to press my hand to his chest, feeling the rapid thud of his heart against my palm. "I love you. Don't you dare fucking leave me to keep me safe. *This* is the only place I want to be. The only place I feel safe is with the three of you. If I lost you, I—"

My torrent of words ended in a gasp as Misael palmed the back of my head and crashed his lips against mine. His kiss was fierce and hot, an answer to everything I'd just said, and I met each stroke of his tongue with my own.

I could taste salt on his lips, and I realized belatedly that he'd been crying. That realization only made me kiss him harder, as if the two of us could heal the wounds in each other just by the connection—the *love*—between us.

Keeping his lips pressed to mine, he rose up onto his knees, pulling me flush against him. And when that wasn't enough, he looped an arm around my waist and stood, nearly lifting me off my feet as he pulled me up with him. We groped at each other desperately, stumbling sideways and bumping into a wall as we made our way down the corridor.

I wasn't sure where we were going, and I didn't much care. I just needed to get this boy into a room with a fucking door.

When I felt a doorknob at my back, I reached for it blindly, and Misael and I spilled into what turned out to be a bathroom. He shut the door behind us, and I was vaguely aware of him turning the lock on the knob as I scrambled for the button of his pants.

He was already hard for me, his cock straining against the fabric, and he groaned when I unzipped him and slipped my hand inside. Then he grabbed both sides of my face, his fingers threading through my hair as he drew back a few inches to stare at me.

I gazed back at him, my chest heaving as I breathed hard and fast. I gripped his cock through the fabric of his boxers, and I could feel it throb against my palm. I moved my hand up and down, and his nostrils flared as his grip on me tightened. His eyes bounced back and forth between mine, and his breath tickled my face.

"I love you too, Cora. I've never loved anyone like I love you."

His words were thick with emotion, and I believed every one of them, all the way down to my soul.

"So you won't ever leave me?" I pressed, still working his cock in hard strokes.

"Fuck," he gritted out. "No fuckin' way, Coralee. Never."

Then he dropped his head, stealing the breath from my lungs with a kiss that made the world around me seem to spin. He walked me backward, hands still gripping my face, until my ass hit the edge of the sink. I kicked off my borrowed shoes just before he hoisted me up onto it, sliding his hands down my legs to wrap them around his body.

His cock pressed against my core, and a breathless whimper fell from my lips as the thick length rubbed right where I needed it most. My heels dug into his ass, urging him closer even as I wrenched my lips away from his and gasped, "Dress! Off!"

With a low growl in the back of his throat, Misael groped for the zipper at the back of the dress. As he tugged it down, revealing more and more of my bare skin to the cool air, I moaned greedily. His hand delved inside the split in the fabric, running over my back and down my spine. Then he stepped back and grabbed the hem, and I shifted my weight, allowing him to pull it off and over my head.

It hit the ground a second later, and Misael's lips were already on the swell of my breast, tracing the line of my bra with his tongue. My nipples pressed against the soft fabric, already so sensitive that it was almost painful. And when he dipped his head lower and drew one tender bud between his teeth, I clamped my lips together to drown my cry of pleasure. His mouth closed around my bra-covered breast, and when he began to suck in long pulls, I arched against him, demanding more.

He gave it.

One large hand delved into my other bra cup, finding my peaked and waiting nipple. He tugged and rolled it between his fingers, making me throw my head back as a new wave of sensation shocked my nerve endings.

I couldn't wait. I loved this boy, and fear of losing him still echoed in my heart. I needed to feel him inside me. Needed to be viscerally connected to him before I could believe that I hadn't lost him already.

That he was mine.

That he would *stay* mine, come what may.

I tore at his shirt, shoving it up his chest until he let me haul it over his head. The second it was off, my hands were on him again, gliding over the smooth, warm skin of his chest until I reached the waistband of his pants. I pushed them down, reaching down with my other hand to free his cock from the confines of his boxers as I did.

God, I wanted to put my mouth on him. I wanted to drop to my knees and worship him, to make him look down at me with peace and happiness and desire in his eyes. I wanted to be his dirty angel, his filthy savior.

But right now, I wanted to feel him inside me more.

As he released my breast, leaving a wet mark around my nipple from his mouth, I urged him closer, rubbing his cock lightly and making him grunt.

I released him only long enough to fist the crotch of my panties, tugging the material aside.

"Please, Misael," I whispered as he kissed me again. "Fuck me. I need you to fuck m—"

I didn't even finish the last word before he complied.

He drove inside me, his first thrust so hard it seemed to knock the air from my lungs. Misael was usually playful and sweet, even in bed. But this? This was something different. This was something as primal and instinctive as humanity itself, something that existed in our blood even now, no matter how civilized we pretended to be.

A feral impulse to claim.

To mark.

To *own*.

There was nothing gentle or tender about his movements, but I felt the love in them anyway. That was something I had never known until I'd met the Lost Boys—something they had taught me.

Sometimes love wasn't soft.

Sometimes it was hard, almost brutal.

But my body recognized and responded to this kind of love as surely as it did sweet kisses and light caresses. In fact, I craved this kind of contact.

Every time Misael bottomed out inside me, so deep it almost hurt, his pelvis slammed against my clit, making sparks shoot through me. One of his hands held my thigh in a bruising grip, keeping me right where he wanted me, while the other looped around my back, supporting me as he drove into me again and again.

"I love you, Coralee. I fuckin' *need* you." His words were broken and choppy, harsh and breathless. "Come for me. Come all over me."

As if he couldn't hold back any longer, he plunged inside me one last time, grinding his hips against mine in a rough circle as he let out a choked grunt. His cock pulsed as he flooded me with his cum, and I did just what he'd asked.

I came all over him.

My whole body shuddered, my core clenching as a gush of my own wetness flooded from the place where his cock impaled me. I buried my face in his neck, sobbing out my release as it poured through me like fire. It was too much, a pleasure so overwhelming it threatened to steal my senses. I bit down hard on his warm skin, closing my eyes and losing myself entirely in the feeling of Misael.

We were connected so deeply I couldn't tell where I ended and he began. I was wrapped around him, and he was wrapped around me, our souls knitting together so tightly that I thought it would kill me to tear us apart.

The tension finally drained from my body as the orgasm released me from its high, but I kept my hold on Misael. My arms were wrapped around him, my teeth still clamped around his skin as I breathed hot and wet against his neck. But I couldn't bear to let even that connection go.

Finally, when my heartbeat began to slow, I lifted my head from the crook of his neck, peering down at my handiwork. The impression of two rows of teeth were clearly visible, with a growing hickey blossoming in between them. Instead of any sort of embarrassment, fierce pride and possessiveness surged through me, and I dropped my head again to lap at his skin, licking my bite mark like a cat.

Misael chuckled, his hands gliding over my thighs and ass. "Did you mark me, Princess?"

"No," I said, unable to hide the smile in my voice as I licked him again.

He laughed. "You're a shit liar, you know that?"

Lifting one of his hands from my ass, he gripped my hair and pulled my head up so he could meet my eyes. The pleased arousal sparking in his deep brown irises made me clench around him again.

"It's okay. I like knowin' I'll be walkin' around tomorrow with your mark on me. I hope the whole damn world sees it. Let 'em know I belong to you."

"I belong to you too, Misael," I murmured, pulling against his grip on my hair to kiss him again. "Marked or not. I'm yours."

I could feel his smile against my lips, both sinful and sweet.

"I know."

FIFTEEN

I COULD'VE STAYED in the bathroom with Misael until well after the dinner party was over, but that was probably a bad idea for several reasons. Everyone had seen how upset Misael was when he'd bolted from the table, so I was sure no one expected us back all that soon. But if we took too long, someone would eventually come looking for us—and Nathaniel still intimidated me enough that I had no desire to get caught having sex in his bathroom.

We held each other and kissed for a few more minutes, indulging in the softer side of love alongside the harder one. Then Misael reluctantly pulled out of me.

He cleaned me up, his touch careful and gentle, before helping me down from the sink counter. We got dressed slowly, eye-fucking each other the whole time. Even though we'd only gotten partially undressed to start with, Misael looked sexy as hell with his shirt off, his pants slung low on his hips, and his cock jutting out, bobbing slightly with every movement. I almost gave in to the impulse I'd had earlier and dropped to my knees in front of him. He'd barely softened at all, and I was sure I could coax another orgasm out of him easily.

But I worried more about *him* getting in trouble with Nathaniel than me, so I resisted the urge. We needed to get back to the dinner.

I did step forward to kiss him once before we left the bathroom though, pressing my palms against his chest and feeling the steady rhythm of his heart inside.

"I love you," I whispered. I wanted to say it a hundred times over, to imprint it on his soul.

"Love you more," he murmured against my lips.

I grinned. There was no way that could be true, but I liked the way the words sounded as they came out of his mouth, so I decided not to argue that point with him.

"Are you okay?" I asked as I pulled back.

We'd gotten so lost in each other that we hadn't finished our conversation about his father—Claudio. About what all of this meant for Misael, and about how he was taking it.

"I will be."

He gave me a lopsided smile, taking my hand as he reached for the door. I could tell he meant it, but I could also see the confusion and pain in his eyes, even though he tried to hide it behind his usual cheer.

I squeezed his hand.

He would be okay. I'd make sure of it.

When we arrived back in the dining room, the conversation lulled as everyone looked up at us. Misael flushed slightly, avoiding Claudio's gaze as he walked me to my spot at the table and pulled my chair out for me. I couldn't help letting my own gaze flick toward the man across from us, and I caught him watching Misael with an expression of regret mingled with hope, and something like approval.

Well, if he was proud of who his son had turned out to be, he should be. I wasn't sure I was willing to forgive him for the circumstances Misael had had to overcome to turn into the wonderful person he was today though. What might his life have been like if he hadn't been parentless since the age of six?

There was a little voice in my head that said if Misael's upbringing had been different, if he hadn't been put into the foster system when he was young, he never would've met the other Lost Boys. He never would've met me.

I couldn't bear to think about that, and I didn't know quite how to make peace with the fact that if his father hadn't abandoned his mother, all of our lives would be unrecognizable right now.

Maybe wishing for the past to be different was always a bad idea. In the aftermath of Dad's arrest, I had prayed more times than I could count for it all to be a dream. I'd wished I would wake up back in my old bed and realize none of it had been real.

But if I'd gotten my wish, I would've missed out on the best thing that'd ever happened to me.

Misael settled back into his seat, and the rest of dinner passed without incident. Claudio didn't bring up the subject again, and by the end of the meal, he put down his empty glass of scotch and turned to face Nathaniel.

"I understand what an honor it is to be approached by you. And I understand the benefits a partnership has. But I'm not unaware that you'd benefit plenty from any alliance between us too. My organization is young. My men are dedicated and loyal. And we're growing. Month by month, year by year, we'll keep growing." He smiled lightly. "I'm sure you've thought of that."

Nathaniel nodded, keeping his expression impassive. "I have."

"There are a few guys on my team who think I'm foolish to even consider this," Claudio acknowledged, grimacing slightly. "But I *am* considering it. I'll have my answer for you soon."

"Good."

Nathaniel didn't pressure Claudio for a more detailed answer, and it occurred to me that the Lost Boys' boss really did want this alliance to happen. So much so that he wasn't willing to risk pushing too hard or forcing Claudio's hand. Luke Carmine must be a bigger threat than I'd realized if Nathaniel was so interested in teaming up against him.

Claudio turned to Misael, addressing him directly for the first time since we'd arrived back at the table.

"You know where to find me. Please come visit sometime. I'll answer any questions you like."

His words were a little stiff, and I got the feeling there was so much more he wanted to say. Things he *would've* said, if not for the fact that this entire thing had become way more public than he probably wanted. If he'd had any other choice about where to approach Misael, he probably would've taken it.

Misael didn't answer, just dipped his head once, acknowledging he'd heard the man.

Now that I knew Claudio was his father, I could see the resemblance between them. It must've been what'd tipped Claudio off. They both had fine, angular features, defined jaw lines, and full lips. They both moved with the same sort of easy grace, and even their smiles were similar.

Wrenching my attention away from the man who had declared himself to be Misael's father, I stood along with everyone else, finding myself immediately surrounded by my boys.

"Come for a drink in my study," Nathaniel told Claudio, jerking his chin toward a door on the far side of the room. Then his gaze shifted to the Lost Boys, landing on Misael last. "You're dismissed for the night. Thank you all."

There was no anger in his tone, and I got the feeling his dismissal of them was more to give Misael a way out than because he was displeased with how the evening had gone.

He and Claudio disappeared into the study, and Josephine led us all to the door. She surprised me again my hugging Misael, and I realized that whether any of us acknowledged it or not, the boys had sort of become her surrogate sons. And me her surrogate daughter.

I didn't mind it though, and even though Misael stiffened awkwardly in her hug before gingerly patting her back, I was grateful for her gesture of support. Just like she had done with me upstairs, she was making sure he knew he wasn't alone.

Someone had left my school clothes folded neatly on a chest in the entryway, and as Josephine picked them up and handed them to me, she said, "Keep the dress. It's yours."

Shit. I'd been hoping she would forget that plan. Not that I didn't like the dress—I loved it more than any other dress I'd ever worn—but I felt bad taking it from her. But I didn't reject her generosity, thanking her as she bustled us toward the door.

It was cold outside, and as soon as we got in the car, Bishop turned the heat up on high then wrapped his hand around mine, warming me with his touch. As he cranked the wheel one-handed and pulled out onto the street, Kace gave a low grunt in the back seat.

"That was some fuckin' night."

"You okay?" Bish asked, glancing into the rearview mirror to catch Misael's gaze.

"Yeah," Misael said, giving the same half-true response he'd given me. Then he shook his head. "I can't believe he fuckin' *left* her."

"But he did it because he loved her." Bishop's voice was

low, and I could hear how much he wanted to fix this for Misael. It made my heart ache sweetly. "That's not nothin'."

"Yeah." Misael lapsed into a thoughtful silence, then he asked, "Should I go visit him?"

"Like he asked?" Bishop shrugged. "Why not? At the very least, you can get answers. Fill in all the missing details. Find out more about your mom. Then if you decide you want to hate the fucker, you can do it without havin' to wonder. You'll know the whole story."

I saw Misael nod through the reflection in the side-view mirror. "True. Besides, I bet Nathaniel will want me to go. He's still tryin' to secure this whole partnership between them. If I can help him with that, I should."

I bristled inwardly, not liking the idea that Nathaniel would try to leverage one of his people's personal life into a bargaining chip. But then again, he hadn't specifically told Misael to do that. The dark-haired boy was just assuming that's what he would want.

Bishop brought me back to Highland Park so I could get my car, and I practically crawled into the back seat as I kissed Kace and Misael goodbye. I licked Misael's hickey once more for good measure, drawing out the first full smile I had seen on his face all evening. Then I leaned over the center console and kissed Bishop.

"You're good for us, Coralee," he whispered, catching my wrist before I could pull back. His voice was so low I knew it was meant only for me. "We need you."

My stomach gave a strange sort of flip-flop at his words. I loved hearing him say that, although it scared me a little.

I was still promised to someone else. My life was still bound up in the demands of my father.

But that didn't make Bishop's words any less true.

They needed me.

And I needed them.

They watched me get into my car and followed me partway back to my house like a secret service detail before finally splitting off and heading back to the other side of the city.

When I pulled into the large garage at my parents' house, it was nearly ten o'clock, later than I had planned on staying out. Prom committee meetings didn't usually last seven hours, and I hoped like hell my dad would buy some other excuse for my prolonged absence.

I scooted the seat back and awkwardly changed back into my school clothes, then stashed the dress I'd gotten from Josephine in the trunk. I'd come back for it later.

The entryway was dimly lit when I stepped inside the house, and I tried to ignore the heavy drumming of my heart as I crept through the mansion. I made sure to avoid Dad's office, skirting around it just in case he was up late working.

I padded quietly up the stairs, but when I reached the top, I almost missed the last step.

My father stood at the end of the hallway, where it veered off toward the east wing where he and Mom slept. I almost hadn't noticed him because he was standing still and quiet several yards away, but now I couldn't drag my gaze from his.

Fuck.

Fear rattled through me. I expected him to come barreling toward me, to grab my arm and berate me like he had at the restaurant.

But he didn't.

He didn't move or speak.

I stood frozen for three long heartbeats, trying to read his expression in the dim light. Then I turned away and hurried to my room before he could stop me.

Dammit. He knows.

So why hadn't he done anything?

SIXTEEN

THE NEXT FEW WEEKS WERE... surreal.

My father knew about the Lost Boys. He'd seen evidence of their existence on the security feed from the pool house, and I was certain he knew they were the ones I snuck off to meet with every time I said I was staying late at school for a prom committee meeting or going out with friends.

But he never said anything.

He didn't ground me again.

He completely ignored it, as if everything was perfectly fine.

The plans for my wedding to Barrett progressed, and my father seemed determined to make it happen. He had made sure the guest list would be packed with important figures in his social circle, people he wanted to impress or intimidate. So maybe he had decided that as long as the marriage went through, he didn't give a fuck how many boys I had on the side. That was essentially what Barrett had said when he'd told me he had no plans to stop fucking other women after we were married.

But that wouldn't work for me. I didn't want the Lost Boys, the boys I loved, to be on the side of anything. Not to mention the fact that they were all dominating and fiercely possessive. They shared me with each other because they loved and trusted each other, but there was no way in hell they would share me with another man—even if I had wanted that, which I most certainly didn't.

The wedding wouldn't happen.

I had become fixated on that single thought, repeating it over and over to myself as a way of getting through each day.

There was no way I could go through with it, but that still didn't solve the problem of how to get out of it without risking the boys. My father was stubborn and demanding, and my past several interactions with him had shown me that the harder I fought against him, the more his grip tightened.

So I needed to find a way to negotiate my way out of this. To make him think it was his idea, that there was benefit to *him* in calling off the wedding between me and Barrett.

I thought about trying to track down Muse again to see if there was any damaging information on the King family I could get my hands on. After spending several months in prison, I didn't think my dad would like the idea of attaching himself to a family that was likely to topple.

And I kept pulling out the sheets of paper I had printed in Dad's office and staring at them, wondering how I could use them. Would he respond to blackmail? Would he let me out of this if I threatened to expose him?

I wasn't sure what I had was enough to fully implicate him though. And if it wasn't, all it would do was alert him to what I knew and unleash his fury at me.

So, I waited.

And worried.

School days were a blur of sullen faces and glares. No one openly taunted me anymore, but I had been written off entirely by most of the student population. If I still cared about playing their fucking games and trying to climb the social ladder, maybe becoming an outcast would've hurt. But I wanted no part of that bullshit anymore.

The one bright spot was the fact that, without my dad breathing down my neck, I was able to sneak away to visit the Lost Boys sometimes. I wanted to spend every second with them, but I didn't want to push my unusually good luck, so I only ventured to their neighborhood a couple times a week.

Misael had decided to take his father up on his offer, and the rest of us went with him the first time he went back to the club to see Claudio. I stuck close by Misael's side, joining the other two boys in glaring down Claudio as if daring him to fucking mess with us—to even think about hurting his son.

But the man with the friendly eyes and the tattoos seemed earnest enough. More and more, I believed that he'd had no knowledge of Misael's existence, and I could see a heaviness in his expression when he spoke about it that made me think it was something he would never make peace with. Something he would never stop blaming himself for.

As the bitter winter air slowly began to warm into spring sunshine, we visited Claudio a few more times, and every time we did, I could sense Misael's walls coming down a little bit more. It wasn't in his nature to trust, or to believe in pretty words or promises. But Claudio was so steadfast in his insistence that he wanted to make things right, never wavering in that for a second, and I could tell that Misael was slowly beginning to believe.

I was glad.

I may never entirely forgive Claudio, but I couldn't find it in me to hate him either. Truthfully, he could've kept his suspicions to himself, never stepping forward to claim that he was Misael's father, and no one would've been the wiser. The fact that he hadn't done that went a long way toward proving how much he wanted to be in Misael's life.

None of the Lost Boys had happy histories, and although my upbringing had been vastly different than theirs, I didn't exactly have a good one either. It seemed like the universe owed at least one of us a good parent.

A grin crossed my face as I stepped out of the shower, my thoughts turning to our last visit with Claudio. I wiped off the condensation on the glass and ran my fingers through my wet blonde hair. But when I wrapped a towel around myself and stepped into the bedroom to grab fresh clothes, the smile melted from my face.

Poppy was in my room. So was my mother.

They were speaking in low tones as Poppy rifled through a selection of dresses hanging on a garment rack and Mom ran an assessing gaze over each one.

My hands clutched at the towel I wore, my brows drawing together. "What the hell are you doing in here?"

"Language, Cordelia," Mom said sharply. She was dressed elegantly, hair and makeup styled to perfection as usual, even though it was just nine in the morning on a Saturday.

"What are you doing?" I repeated.

"What does it look like?" She blinked up at me, appearing honestly surprised. "I'm choosing a prom dress for you."

Prom. Fuck.

Despite the number of "prom committee meetings" I'd gone to over the past month, I had completely forgotten that the actual event was coming up.

"I'm not going to prom," I said shortly, veering toward my closet even as my heart picked up its pace.

"Of course you are, dear. With Barrett. What would it look like if two soon-to-be newlyweds didn't go to the most important social event at the school all year?"

"It would look like they don't actually like each other," I gritted out, wheeling around to face her. I hadn't spoken to my mother much since the day of my engagement party—the day I'd realized she would take my father's side over mine every time—but I still vividly remembered our last interaction in this room.

I wanted to leap at her again. I wanted to tear the dresses off the rack and shred them into pretty, colorful ribbons.

Maybe Mom could tell what I was thinking, because something almost like fear flickered in her eyes, as if she were dealing with a rabid animal that might attack at any minute. But she pressed her lips together, taking a dress from Poppy and stepping forward.

"You're going, Cordelia. This is *not* open for debate. Your father has been lenient on you lately because he expects you to obey when it matters, and this is one of the times when it matters."

"Yeah?" I shot back, my anger growing. "Did he tell you that in one of your little heart-to-hearts? Oh wait, I forgot, you still hardly even speak to each other!"

Her nostrils flared wide, and I could see hurt and resentment flash across her face. "What goes on between me and your father is none of your business."

"Of course not." I shook my head, a sneer curling my lips. "You're just my fucking parents."

"Language!"

Her voice cracked like a whip, silencing me momentarily. She looked furious, and I realized that I'd hit a deeper nerve than I had thought.

She had cheated on my father while he was in prison, but she hadn't done it for love. She had done it to secure herself some of the creature comforts she missed from when we'd had money. She had done it as a bargaining tool.

Now that my father was back home and we had our

wealth and power back, she was by his side again. Maybe
she'd even thought they could go back to the way things used
to be.

But it was too late. She'd shown her true colors.

She'd shown that she would always put her own self-
interests above others. That she would abandon someone the
instant that person could no longer help her, and that she
didn't even know the meaning of loyalty.

*It's a shame she and Dad don't get along anymore. They're
fucking perfect for each other.*

That bitter thought filtered through my mind as Mom
stepped toward me and thrust the dress into my hands.

"Poppy will help you dress and prepare," she said stiffly.
"Barrett will come pick you up at 7:30. Be ready, or you'll be
grounded until you graduate."

With that, she turned on her heel and stalked out, leaving
Poppy gazing at me with a mixture of awkwardness and pity.

Pick your battles, Cora.

I clenched my jaw, repeating the words over and over in
my head. I still had half a mind to shred the dress and tell
Mom to go fuck herself. But if I was grounded, I wouldn't be
able to see the boys for weeks. I couldn't risk that.

"I don't need your help. I can get ready myself," I told
Poppy, wishing like hell she were Ava. I wanted someone I
could trust, someone I could lean on for a little bit of
comfort, although not even Ava could've helped me out of
this mess.

"But, Miss—"

"I'm fine. I'll tell Mom I sent you away. You won't get in trouble."

Indecision warred on her face for a moment, but she finally nodded and slunk out. I tossed the dress on the bed, glaring at the expensive blue fabric with the beaded bodice and ombre skirt. I still had several hours before I needed to put it on, and I wasn't going to wear it a second longer than necessary.

The dress taunted me all day, and I found myself pacing my room like a trapped animal. I skipped dinner, partly because I had no appetite and partly because I had no desire to see either of my parents. At 7:15, I threw on the dress, piled my hair into a rough updo, and brushed on some lip gloss and mascara. Fuck Mom if she thought I was going to do more than that for this bullshit.

When I couldn't delay the inevitable anymore, I trotted down the stairs quickly, my heels sounding like gunshots on the polished marble. Barrett was standing in the large entry room talking to my father, and my footsteps slowed at the sight of them. My skin felt cold and clammy, and the soft fabric of my dress suddenly felt scratchy and too-tight.

Keeping my chin raised high, I stalked forward. Barrett was dressed in a bespoke suit that might've even made him look handsome—but I couldn't see any of that anymore. All I saw when I looked at him was the slimy monster underneath.

"Ah, Cordelia. There you are." My dad turned to me, smiling widely as if any of this was okay. "I hope you two have a wonderful time. Don't forget to get pictures. And since it's prom night, I'll allow you to stay out a bit later."

I just stared at him, not even able to summon a snarky response to that. Every single word he'd said had been like a dagger in my heart, yet he smiled at me as if expecting the lies he lived by to alter reality.

This wasn't okay. Nothing would make it okay.

So I didn't say anything. I just stepped toward the door, not even caring if Barrett followed me or not.

The ride to school was as uncomfortably painful as riding in a hearse—to your own funeral. The driver ignored us, and I ignored Barrett, determined to talk to him as little as possible this evening.

When we arrived at Highland Park, the entire school was lit up, and a red carpet was laid down out front as if this were a movie premiere or something. Girls gathered together in tight groups, exclaiming over each other's dresses as the guys they'd come with laughed and joked among themselves. We slid from the car, and Barrett tried to take my arm, but I yanked it away.

"Don't fucking touch me," I hissed.

Irritation flashed in his face, and he looked around quickly to see if we'd drawn any attention. I could see him weighing the pros and cons of forcing the issue, wondering whether it was worth it to make a scene trying to teach me my place.

It wouldn't be. I'd make sure of that.

The vicious smile that quirked my lips must've given

away my thoughts, because Barrett let out a low noise of
disgust and settled for walking a few inches to one side of me
as we entered the school.

The girl I'd been just a year ago might've been happy to
be here. She might've been glad to be seen on the arm of the
son of one of the most powerful families in Baltimore. She
would've been among the groups of girls whispering together,
complimenting each other's dresses, admiring each other's
jewelry.

The girl I was today took one look around and marched
toward the drink table, wishing there was something to spike
the fucking punch with.

Minutes ticked by as more and more students arrived,
and the lights in the gymnasium were dimmed as music
blared through the space. Barrett stood awkwardly at my side
for a while, casting me glances out of the corners of his eyes
every now and then.

Finally, he turned to me. "Would you like to dance?"

I looked over at him slowly, brows pulling together. "No."

He scoffed, then shook his head. "You think you're being
so tough, saying 'no, no, no' over and over? Well, let me break
it to you, sweetheart. You're not. All you're doing is acting
like a fucking baby, whining about how this isn't what you
want." He turned to face me fully, and he reminded me so
much of my father for an instant that I fell back a step. "This
is happening. You're not stopping it by being a fucking bitch
every step of the way. I think you know that. So why don't
you climb off your fucking high horse, come to grips with

reality, and dance with me. Your parents want pictures, remember?"

He smirked as he said the last bit, and something inside me snapped.

No, not snapped.

Tore.

It was as if someone had taken the two halves of me, the two sides I'd spent the past months trying to reconcile, and physically torn them apart. A deep ache spread through my chest, radiating outward as if the tear in my being had left me bleeding internally.

"You're wrong." My voice was so low I could barely hear it over the music, thick with emotion. "You're so fucking wrong. I will *never* be yours. You're a smarmy, greasy, ugly-souled hypocrite who thinks the world *owes* you more than the wealth and power you were lucky enough to be born into. There are people who love me who would never forgive me for saying this, but I'll die before I marry you. I fucking mean it."

My hands shook as I turned on my heel, wanting to get as far away from Barrett as possible. But before I could walk away, he grabbed my wrist.

"What the hell, Cora? You can't just—"

I yanked my arm free and shoved at his chest, and his eyes flew wide as he caught his balance. I hit him again, my hands curled into fists this time, and several people around us stepped back, their eyes widening.

Barrett's body tensed, like he was going to retaliate or

grab me again. But his gaze flicked around the room, realizing how much attention we'd already drawn, and he slowly took a step back, his eyes burning into mine.

"Get your rebellious phase out of the way now, Cora," he drawled, a cruel smile curving his lips. "Because the first thing I'm going to do when we get married is teach you some fucking manners."

A burst of cold fear tried to break through the anger pulsing inside my veins, but I could barely register it. All I saw was red. Turning away from the boy I despised more than almost anyone in the world, I stalked away, scanning the edges of the gymnasium as I looked for someplace quiet and dark to pass the rest of the evening.

My skin prickled, a sudden awareness making my whole body buzz.

I froze, my feet stopping in place so I could inspect the edges of the room more carefully.

My heart beat hard and fast when I recognized the broad frame of the boy with short blond hair who stood just inside one of the doors that led to the courtyard outside.

Kace.

SEVENTEEN

MY ENTIRE BODY reacted to the sight of him, and I glanced behind him, searching for the other two Lost Boys. I didn't see them though. Kace was alone.

What was he doing here?

How much of my fight with Barrett had he seen?

Sudden fear swept through me, and my feet started moving toward him before I even consciously gave them the command. Kace had a bigger heart than almost anyone I knew. But he'd been raised on violence, and he was protective and possessive of the things he loved. If he had seen Barrett grab my wrist, seen him manhandle me like that...

Fuck.

I couldn't let Kace get into a fight on Highland Park grounds. If shit went down between the two of them, Barrett would get his ass handed to him—but he'd be only too fucking happy to press charges.

I was practically running by the time I reached Kace and threw myself into his arms. He was so solid and big that he didn't even stagger at the collision, and although he stayed still, I could feel his heart beating hard against mine.

"What are you doing here?" I whispered.

He didn't answer. I looked up to see his gaze focused over my shoulder, and I was positive he was staring at Barrett.

No. I needed him with *me*.

Kace had killed a man for me, and I didn't doubt he would do it again if he had to. But violence wouldn't help either of us in this situation. It would only make things worse.

So I fought against the violence brewing inside him with the only thing I could think of.

Love.

Rising up onto my tiptoes, I looped one hand around the back of Kace's neck and pressed my lips to his, relishing how hard he was everywhere—how soft he made me feel. His earthy sage scent crept into my nostrils as his arms wrapped around me and he returned the kiss with wild heat.

Then, before I could even register what was happening, his lips broke apart from mine. I had a horrible certainty that he was about to push past me and stalk toward Barrett like a killing machine. But instead, the world spun around me as I was picked up by the waist and thrown over Kace's shoulder.

I let out a little yelp as his arm beaded around my thighs, pinning them against him as he began walking toward one of the other doors on the perimeter of the room. He shoved it open, and the lights and sound of the dance faded as it closed behind us. The hallway was dark, and the sound of Kace's heavy footfalls seemed like drumbeats in the empty corridor.

My cheeks flamed as a rush of heat surged through my body. On the one hand, half my school had just watched this boy throw me over his shoulder and carry me out of the room like a caveman claiming his mate.

On the other hand...

I fucking wanted to be claimed.

My core throbbed as heat pooled in my lower belly. I could feel the flex of Kace's muscles beneath me as he walked, and the sheer strength and power of his body made me ache for more contact. I wanted to be enveloped by him. Owned by him.

When he finally set me down, I found myself leaning back against a door. My legs wobbled a little, adjusting to supporting my weight as I gazed up at the tall boy before me. His hands rested on the door on either side of my head, and he was staring down at me with an intensity that almost burned, his moss-green eyes seeming darker than usual in the dim light.

He dropped his head, our noses almost brushing as I tilted my own head up. Then he kissed me again, and my whole world narrowed to the connection between us. I was vaguely aware of him doing something with the door handle, but I couldn't focus on that. Not when his tongue was sliding so insistently against mine, not when I could feel the heat radiating from his body, lighting mine up like a furnace.

Then the door suddenly fell away from behind me as it

swung open. I'd been resting so much of my weight against it that I almost fell over when it opened, but Kace's arms caught me, holding me tight to him as he walked me backward into the room.

I expected it to be a bathroom. He and I had made something of a habit of fucking in public bathrooms on school grounds, so it only seemed fitting that we would christen one of the bathrooms at Highland Park too.

But when Kace tore his lips from mine and began working them along the line of my jaw and down my neck, I blinked my eyes open and realized I'd been wrong.

We were in the nurse's office.

It was a small, sterile room with an exam table in the middle and stacks of brochures on the small stand by the door.

Keeping his lips on my skin, Kace urged me backward again, and when my ass bumped into the exam table, he kept moving my upper body backward, dipping me deeply as his hand supported the back of my head. His lips trailed over my chest, along the neckline of my dress, and he made a pleased, animalistic sound in his throat.

It was the closest he'd come to speaking since he'd arrived here.

I groaned, reaching up to grab handfuls of his short blond hair, arching my back even more to encourage his exploration. "Fuck, Kace!"

"I want to kill him, Princess."

The words were muttered low, spoken against my skin as

he devoured me, but I could hear the truth in them. I could *feel* the truth in his body, in the tension that tightened every one of his muscles.

"Don't!" I gasped. Forcing my head up, I met his gaze as his lips brushed over the exposed tops of my breasts, staring into his eyes as if I was trying to meld our souls into one. "Please, Kace. He's not fucking worth it. Stay with me. Show me I'm yours."

Something shifted in his expression, brutal anger warring with insatiable hunger. His breathing grew harsh, and the hand that roamed my body became rougher, more possessive.

"Are you mine, Princess? Are you ours? Do you belong to us?"

"Yes," I breathed, shifting my head to the side, wanting more of his mouth and hands everywhere. "Yours. All of me."

He drew back slightly, the muscles in his neck standing out like thick cords. His tongue slid out to lick his full lower lip, and my core clenched, a flood of anticipation moving through my body.

"All of you," he repeated slowly.

Then, for the second time in one night, I was moved so quickly that the world spun in my vision. But this time, I wasn't picked up and thrown over Kace's shoulder. This time, I was spun around so that my front side was facing the exam table. I sucked in a breath as Kace's arms wrapped around my waist like two pythons, pinning me against his large frame.

"*All* of you," he breathed in my ear, the word raspy and raw. His cock was hard. I could feel it through the fabric of my skirt, pressing against me urgently, insistently, like a warning.

"Yes."

The word was a low gasp, and when one of his hands slid down between my thighs, I ground against it.

"Then I'm going to take what's mine, Princess."

Even as he spoke, his other arm released me, and he began gathering the fabric of my skirt in his grip, hauling it up so the hem brushed against the backs of my legs. Higher. Higher.

When the cool air of the room drifted over my exposed ass, Kace drew in a ragged breath. "Bend over."

I did as he commanded without thought, my legs shaking slightly as desire and nerves roiled inside me.

I knew what he was going to do.

What I'd begged him to do. What I'd wanted so badly that night in the pool.

He was going to fuck my ass.

My stomach clenched at the thought, my whole body going rigid. Jesus. He barely fit in my tiny pussy. How was I ever going to take him in my back hole?

Maybe he sensed the sudden change in me, because Kace's touch, while still demanding and possessive, became gentler. He pressed between my shoulder blades, urging me down farther, and when I complied, he slid his hand down my back.

My cheek pressed against the cool, smooth surface of the table, and my hands gripped the edges of it like I needed to hold on to stay upright. My entire body felt like a live wire as Kace draped the gathered fabric of my dress over my lower back, leaving my ass and legs totally exposed.

His palms slid over my rounded curves, squeezing and massaging my flesh, and as he touched me, the hottest fucking noises I'd ever heard spilled from his lips. They were low, incoherent, barely even sounds at all. They were animalistic and primal, and they made my inner walls clench so hard that my clit throbbed.

A gush of wetness dampened my panties, and I knew Kace noticed it, because he stopped moving for a second. Staring at me. Staring at the dark spot spreading over the crotch of my panties.

"Is that for me, Princess?" he murmured, still running his hands over me, his calloused palms sliding over my skin. "Is that cream for me?"

His fingertips dipped inside my panties, smearing the wetness over my folds before dragging it down my thighs. I was breathing harder, and more wetness seeped from me as that one small touch sent my pulse skyrocketing.

"It's always for you."

He growled low in his throat. "Good girl."

Then his fingers slid inside my panties again, and this time, instead of dragging my sticky arousal down my thigh, he slid his fingers upward, teasing my puckered hole.

"You wanted to make sure I'd get you nice and ready, didn't you?" He repeated the gesture, making my ass clench and my legs shake. "You gave me all this cream to make sure you're nice and wet."

"Uh huh," I gasped.

I barely even knew what I was saying anymore. I couldn't concentrate on anything else as his finger slowly worked its way inside my ass. The wetness that he'd coated his fingers with helped him glide inside the tight opening, and the sensation was foreign but... good.

He had gone much deeper than this when I'd been in the pool, but I could tell he was working his way up to it. I was grateful, but when he rotated his finger gently, stretching me out a little more, I couldn't help it. I bumped back against him, seeking more. More sensation, more fullness, more everything.

His other hand, which had been resting on my ass, squeezed hard enough to leave five fingerprints, and I could practically feel him tensing behind me. "Greedy," he muttered, a pleased note in his voice. "So fucking greedy."

"Kace. Please!"

"Fuck."

With no more warning or preamble, he slipped his finger out of me, then shoved my panties down my legs. I was still wearing the heels I'd put on to match my dress, and he made no move to take them off as he slid his hands down my legs and lifted my feet to pull my underwear all the way off.

His lips devoured the skin of my calves, my thighs, the backs of my knees, and it was such an overload of sensation on a place that had never received that much attention before that I found myself panting against the smooth surface of the table, shifting my hips desperately as my hands clenched and unclenched.

I needed release. I needed relief. I was so fucking desperate, so ready to come, so *close*.

"Touch yourself, Coralee." Kace bit down on the swell of my ass cheek, and I jumped. He licked the sting away, then slid one finger through my folds from behind, brushing against my clit as he did. "Make yourself come. Open yourself up for me."

He kept his fingers there as I slowly unwrapped one of my hands from the edge of the table, and when my fingertips found my clit, his joined them. For a moment, we were both touching the little bundle of nerves, our wet fingers sliding together. He placed his over mine and felt the rhythm as I began to massage myself in tight circles, moving fast and hard as I chased the orgasm I needed so badly.

"Fuck, yes. Fuck." He sounded as close to losing it as I was, and he slicked his fingers in my wetness again before bringing them up between my ass cheeks. "Like that, Princess. Fucking come."

And I did. My fingertips blurred on my clit as I tightened and convulsed, pleasure moving through me like an unstoppable wave. As aftershocks made me shudder, I felt the pressure of a fingertip at my back hole, and this time, Kace *did* go deep. He slid in until he felt me tense, then paused a second before pushing in farther.

When he added a second finger, my toes curled inside my

shoes, my back arching as my head came off the table. For a second, the fear returned, but then Kace's large body draped over mine. He brushed the hair off my neck and kissed his way up the side of my throat, brushing his lips over my ear.

"I've got you. I've always got you."

I turned my head, craning my neck to find his mouth and kissing him hard and deep as his second finger joined the first, working slowly into my ass, lubricating and stretching, letting me adjust to the feeling.

It still hurt a bit, but the pain was beginning to fade as adrenaline tore through me, leaving just the feeling of fullness.

The feeling of some unfulfilled promise.

Of intense need.

"Keep touching yourself," he muttered against my lips. "Don't stop. And push back against me."

I did as he commanded. My body was already hungry for another orgasm, and heat began to spread through my lower body as I massaged my aching clit again. I wasn't sure how he knew how to do this so well, how to work with my body and keep me relaxed—and then the sudden, unpleasant thought struck me that even though this was my first time, it might not be his.

A surge of possessive jealousy reared up in me, and I felt a violent need to erase the memories of any other girl from his mind. To wipe them out of existence. To be the only one he ever thought about.

I pushed back against the intrusion of his fingers with my

inner muscles, and when I relaxed, he slid in deeper, moving the two thick digits to stretch me out even more.

My knees were shaking, and I could feel a sheen of sweat covering my skin. My breath was coming in short, choppy pants as an overload of sensations assaulted my nerve-endings.

"Kace! Fuck... Kace!"

My cry was naked and raw as I wrenched my lips away from his, and I didn't give a shit whether he'd locked the door behind us or even whether he'd closed it. All I cared about was the feel of him inside me, the emptiness he was filling with both pleasure and pain.

"Are you ready, Coralee?" he asked, pressing his lips to the corner of my mouth, my cheek, my jaw. His kisses were soft, but the movement of his fingers in my ass had become rougher, making my hips sway forward every time he plunged into me.

"Yes," I grunted. "Yes. Yes."

And then his fingers were sliding out of me, leaving me feeling strangely barren and empty. A second later his clothes rustled, and the sharp hiss of a zipper made goose bumps scatter across my skin. I felt the heat of him behind me before he even touched me, and when his hands fell on my hips, my breath caught.

He held me firmly, his hips pulsing forward as his cock slid between my legs, between my folds, brushing against my fingers as they worked my clit. I could feel him coating himself in my wetness, and I gathered more for him, slipping my fingers inside myself before sliding them over the underside of his thick shaft.

He's so big. He's so fucking big.

A thrill of fear ran through me, but it only heightened my arousal, and as Kace pulled back slightly, my fingers found my clit again, ramping up the need coiling inside me even more.

One of his large hands left my hip, and I could feel him lining himself up, positioning the head of his cock right where I would take him.

Then...

Pressure.

A bite of pain.

Kace's free hand on my hip, his fingers digging into my flesh with a steely grip.

His low grunt, which echoed the same pleasure and pain I was feeling.

"You're so tight. Fuck, you're tight." He was breathing harder too, his body tense as a wire behind me, as if it was taking all his self-control not to snap and surge into me hard and fast. "Push back, Cora. Let me have you. You're fuckin' *mine.*"

The possessiveness in his voice ricocheted through my body, starting at my heart and ending in my clit, and I came again, a rolling orgasm that flowed through me like water.

"Oh, fuck. Yeah, that's it. Just like that."

Kace kept muttering words of praise and encouragement, and both his hands were on my hips again, his tight hold keeping us both steady as my feet shook in my high heels.

I kept coming and coming, and he kept pushing inside, inch by slow inch, until finally, we were completely connected. I could feel his steely thighs pressing against the backs of my legs, feel the texture of his jeans on my sensitive skin, and I drew in a shuddering breath, trying to memorize everything about this moment.

The moment I gave myself entirely to Kace.

His upper body draped over mine again, one hand moving up to capture my jaw as he turned my head so he could kiss me.

"I'm not gonna last long," he muttered when the kiss broke. "You feel too fucking good."

"I don't care," I gasped. This had all been a fucking overload of amazing, new, terrifying sensations anyway. And I had already come three times. Now all I wanted was to feel him come inside me.

"Say 'blue' if it's too much."

Before I could respond to that, Kace drew out partway, his slick cock sliding against my tight walls, then plunged back in, his hips slapping against mine. I gasped but bit down hard on my bottom lip. There was nothing in the world that could make me say "blue" right now.

And I realized just how much restraint Kace had been using before as he finally let go of it.

His body bucked against mine, his hips pistoning hard and fast as he drove into me again and again. Pleasure and pain mingled until they were one and the same, and even though I'd stopped working my clit, I came again anyway.

It was an orgasm unlike any I'd ever had before. It felt like getting ripped apart and fused back together, like I was a star exploding. I threw my head back, and Kace caught the underside of my chin, forcing my back to arch even more. He let out a loud, harsh grunt and then slammed into me one more time, grinding his hips against my ass as he flooded me with his cum.

My whole body shook, the walls of both my core and my ass fluttering desperately.

Breathing hard, Kace wrapped both his arms around me, lifting my torso off the table so we were pressed flush together. His cock was still buried in my ass, and the change of angle made a whole new flood of sensations hit me. Keeping one arm around me, he brushed my messy hair off my face with the other, craning his neck to kiss me.

When he drew back, his moss-green eyes glinted in the dim light coming through the window. His expression was serious, calm... almost peaceful.

"I love you, Coralee," he whispered softly.

EIGHTEEN

I LOVE YOU.

The rush of emotions that rose up in my chest was too much to process, and I sucked in a breath as tears stung my eyes.

"Only you," I said, laughing and crying at the same time, "could tell me that while you're still inside my ass and make it sound romantic."

He smiled broadly, an expression that was so rare on his face that it seemed blinding in the darkness. "Hey. What we just did was extremely romantic."

I laughed again, and the vibrations the sound created in my body seemed to do something to Kace. He groaned, pulling me even closer as he circled his hips against my ass again, his cock pulsing slightly. Then he slowly withdrew, making sure to keep his hands on me so I didn't slump into a heap on the ground.

"Wait here."

He set my hands on the table to brace me up, then crossed to the other side of the room and returned a second later with a few tissues. He gingerly helped clean me up, touching me with such care and ownership that my heart seemed to swell inside my chest. After tossing the tissues away, he slid my panties back on and turned me around, lifting me up to sit on the exam table.

I winced slightly, and concern darkened his features.

"You okay?"

"Yeah." I grinned. "A little sore, but I don't mind."

His hand caught my chin again, tilting my face so he could examine my eyes, as if searching for any hint of a lie. "I didn't hurt you?"

I caught hold of his wrist, biting my lip as I looked at him. How could I explain that even when he *did* hurt me a little, he gave me so much more pleasure than pain? I liked it. I loved the contrast between the two sensations, the way it made me feel electric and alive.

"I didn't say 'blue,' did I?" I asked, my voice teasing. When he didn't look satisfied with that answer, I looped a hand around the back of his neck. "Kace, I love you. And I trust you with everything. My body, my heart, and my soul."

His face stilled, a look almost like shock passing over his features. As if he hadn't expected to hear those words from another human being besides Bishop and Misael in his lifetime.

Well, I would fix that. I would make sure he heard them every day.

"I love you," I said again, just for good measure. But this time, I barely got the words out before he crushed his lips against mine, knocking the breath out of me with the force of his kiss.

We made out for a while in the nurse's office, our hands and lips and tongues unhurried and lazy as we indulged in each other. Just existing in the perfect stillness of this moment.

Finally, Kace pulled back and rested his forehead against mine. "We should get outta here."

"Yeah," I agreed reluctantly.

"I'm not takin' you back to that fuckin' dance."

"Good."

"Bish and Misael had a job to do for Nathaniel that couldn't wait, or they woulda come with me. They dropped me off, but they should be done soon." He pulled his phone out of his back pocket and glanced at the screen. "Scratch that. They're already done. They're on their way."

A grin spread across my face, growing wider and wider.

Instead of having to spend the evening at a prom I never wanted to go to, I was going to spend it with the three boys I loved. And fuck anyone who tried to stop me.

Kace helped me down off the table and kept an arm around my waist as he unlocked and opened the door. I wasn't quite sure how he knew the layout of the school so

well, but he didn't hesitate as he started leading me toward
the front entrance.

But as we passed by the gymnasium, I saw Barrett
striding toward us from the other end of the hall. I tensed
immediately, and his eyes narrowed when he caught sight
of me.

"What the fuck are you doing, Cordelia Van
Rensselaer?" he barked, like I was a wayward child who had
broken a rule. "You think it's acceptable to just walk out on
me like that? I am your date. I am your *fiancé—*"

"No."

I stepped forward, putting my body between him and
Kace. I could practically feel the blond boy behind me,
muscles tensing like a bull preparing to charge. But this time,
I hadn't stepped up because I didn't want Kace to fight. I'd
done it because I didn't *need* him to.

"What?" Barrett's face scrunched up unpleasantly, and
he looked like he'd just swallowed something bitter.

"I said no," I repeated, standing taller. I could still sense
Kace right behind me, a silent support. "It's fucking done,
Barrett. It's over. I don't care what I have to do. I don't care if
my dad cuts off my entire inheritance. I will *never* marry
you."

The boy in front of me blinked a few times, as if his brain
was having a hard time comprehending my words. Then he
let out a choked laugh.

"What, so you'd give up everything for this piece of shit?"
He shifted his gaze behind me, and fury flared hot and

white in my veins. I could feel Kace start to move, but I was way ahead of him. Before he could step around me and punch Barrett, I grabbed the smarmy boy by the shoulders and drove my knee up as hard as I could between his legs.

"Fuuuck!"

The word was wrenched out of him as his body folded in half, his hands flying to his crotch as he tumbled to the floor. My skirt got caught up in his legs and he almost took me with him, but Kace latched an arm around my waist and hauled me away.

The second he set me on my feet, his lips were on mine, hot and hard and demanding. Barrett's groans provided the soundtrack to our kiss, and even though there was nothing particularly romantic about the noise, it hardly mattered. I could feel love and desire flowing through every stroke of Kace's tongue against mine, and I dizzily thought to myself that I would knee Barrett in the balls a hundred more times if it made Kace kiss me like this.

When we broke apart, my "fiancé" was finally starting to crawl to his feet. Kace strode over and put a heavy shoe on his shoulder, then shoved with his foot, sending the boy sprawling again.

Then he turned to me and held out his arm, a beautiful, miraculous grin stretching his lips for the second time tonight. "Ready, Princess?"

"Fuck, yes."

I looped my arm around his, and we strode from the building quickly, bursting through the doors at the front of

the school into the cool night air. We caught sight of Bishop's
car pulling into the lot almost as soon as we stepped outside,
and the two of us made a beeline toward it, racing across the
parking lot and throwing ourselves inside. Bish gunned the
engine and peeled out onto the street, shooting me a curious
sidelong glance as he did.

"What's so funny?"

It wasn't until he asked the question that I realized I was
laughing breathlessly, out of breath and disheveled after
fucking and fighting. I turned to him, feeling the weight that
had been crushing my soul for the past few months
disintegrating. Lifting away. Letting me take a full breath for
the first time in weeks.

"I'm done." I turned sideways so I could face the back
seat too. Kace had heard me say this to Barrett already, but I
wanted him to hear it again. And I wanted Misael to hear. I
wanted them all to know. "I'm done pretending my father
will ever come around. That there'll ever be any way out of
this except the one I'm taking. To just fucking refuse."

Misael's eyes widened, and he leaned forward in his seat.
But Bishop turned to look at me before cutting his gaze back
to the road.

"It won't be that simple, Coralee. You know that, right? I
mean, it's one thing to tell your dad no. It's another thing
entirely to deal with the fallout after you deny him."

For a second, the weight in my chest returned, almost
paralyzing me with worry. That was why I had been so dead-
set on finding another solution—on making Dad think it was

his idea to call off the wedding, and that he was still winning where it counted. Because this? Outright telling him no? It could be dangerous for all of us.

"I know." I reached across the console and grabbed his hand. "But I don't care anymore. Unless you don't want me to—"

"Are you fuckin' kidding?" He squeezed my hand so hard it almost hurt, fire flashing in his eyes as he turned his head to look at me. "Of course we want you to. We're not lettin' that King fucker have what's ours. We just need to make sure you stay safe, is all."

I heard Kace give a grunt of agreement from the backseat, and a second later, Bishop released my hand to reach over and palm the back of my head, dragging me toward him and kissing me hard.

Adrenaline flowed through me, lighting me up from the inside as my lips pressed against his. The ache in my body from Kace's cock, the pain in my knee from hitting Barrett, the speed of the car, and the scent of Bishop's aftershave in my nose—it all made me feel perfectly, wonderfully *alive*.

I gripped Bishop's arm, holding on for dear life as the car sped down the street.

"Alright, alright. Don't fuckin' kill us, Bish," Misael joked from the back seat, and Bishop reluctantly released me, turning to put his attention on the road.

I was breathing harder, my lips tingling, and when Misael leaned around the seat and tilted my head toward his with two fingers on my chin, my greedy mouth found his immediately. I chuckled into the kiss, certain that his words to Bishop earlier had been as much about wanting to do this as about driver safety. I liked that the boys didn't fight over me, but I also liked that they all wanted me and made no secret of that fact.

He ended the kiss and pressed a peck to the tip of my nose, then grinned broadly. "You look hot as fuck in that dress, Coralee. Where do you want to go to celebrate?"

I pursed my lips, considering. Then a smile spread across my face. "Dancing. I want to go dancing."

The atmosphere in the car shifted, seeming to grow hotter. The last time the four of us had gone dancing, I'd ended up having sex with Kace and Misael in the back seat of this very car. Grinding and moving against the three of them on the dance floor had gotten me so worked up we'd barely made it to the car at all before I'd attacked them.

"I like the sound of that," Kace said, his voice taking on a tone that made a shiver run down my spine.

"Me too." Misael cocked an eyebrow at me as he settled back in his seat.

"Dancin' it is, then."

Bish drummed his fingers against the steering wheel, then hung a left onto another street. We were entering Baltimore's more run-down neighborhoods, where the street lights became spottier and more graffiti covered the walls of buildings. The streets were more empty too. We'd have to cut back toward the downtown area to get to any good clubs.

I looked down at my dress. It was a full-length gown,

formal and elegant, and even though it was undeniably beautiful, it didn't exactly look like club-wear. "Do you think I'm overdressed?"

"Nah." Misael chuckled. "Although, hell, I've got a knife on me. If you want, I can modify it for ya before we go in."

A laugh burst out of me as I had a sudden memory of taking a pair of scissors to all the clothes in my closet after my first day at Slateview, in an attempt to fit in better with the other kids there. This time, though, the modifications wouldn't be about putting on a costume. They'd be about removing my bindings. About freeing myself.

"Yeah." I grinned, craning my neck to look at him. "I'd like that."

It was only because I was facing that direction that I saw it—a flash of movement outside the car on the driver's side.

But it didn't matter whether I saw it or not.

Because by the time I did, it was too late.

An engine revved and tires squealed as a car sped toward us from the intersecting side street, and before I could open my mouth to scream or shout a warning, it plowed into Bishop's convertible.

NINETEEN

THE FORCE of the impact felt like being at the epicenter of a bomb. There was a moment of blinding, rushing panic, a noise so loud it seemed to reverberate inside my fucking soul, and then blackness.

Quiet.

Nothingness.

I floated in that hazy space for seconds that felt like hours, and when the world turned back on, all I could hear was the roar of blood in my ears and a sharp ringing sound. My body ached, and something wet trickled down the side of my face. When I reached a hand up to touch it, my fingertips shook so badly it felt like I was having a seizure.

"Bish..." My voice was a low groan. "Kace. Misael?"

Gingerly, I turned my head to look over at them, but as I did, the back window exploded inward. I screamed, ducking on instinct.

"Fuck!"

Bishop's voice was thick with pain and urgent with fear, and he ducked too, reaching across me to pull something from the glove box, then unclipping his seatbelt and mine and shoving my door open.

He pushed me, making me spill out of the car as several loud pops sounded outside and the driver's side window shattered. I hit the pavement in a heap, my bruised body barely able to control my fall as my skirts tangled around my legs.

"Misael? Kace?" Bish called over his shoulder, throwing himself over the console and spilling out of the car after me, pulling me up into a crouch next to the front wheel.

The back passenger door opened, and Kace and Misael threw themselves out. Kace had an arm around Misael's waist, and something dark and shiny ran freely down the dark-haired boy's arm.

Blood.

Oh, fuck.

"We gotta fuckin' go," Kace said quickly, meeting Bishop's gaze.

As if to punctuate his words, several more gunshots rang out in the dark night, and Bishop leaned around the hood of the car to return fire. That's what he'd grabbed from the glove box, I realized. A gun.

As Bishop shot at our attackers, Kace hauled Misael up to a low crouch. "You gotta help him run, Princess. Get rid of your heels."

I nodded, scrambling to kick off my shoes and loop my arm around Misael's waist. Kace pulled a gun from the back of his waistband and braced his arms over the car's trunk, firing off several rounds.

"Go! Go!" Bishop shouted, his weapon still braced in his hands.

I didn't question. I didn't hesitate. I just reacted.

Hauling Misael up, I sprinted away from the car. Thank fuck, the boy beside me hadn't been hit badly enough that he couldn't hold himself upright, and he moved almost as fast as I did, holding out his good hand to point to a large building a little way down the street.

"There!" he yelled.

I moved toward it, and Kace and Bishop ran after us, still shooting at the people who had hit us, holding them off. Shouts and gunfire rang out in the night, loud, angry male voices calling to each other as they pursued us.

A bullet whizzed by my head as we neared the building, and I screamed, ducking as Misael and I both stumbled sideways. Dirt and pebbles dug into my feet as we put on a final burst of speed, slamming into the door hard. I grabbed the handle and yanked, but it wouldn't give.

"Locked!" I shouted, my voice a wild shriek as I pulled harder.

"Move!"

I did as Kace commanded, releasing the handle and stepping sideways, and a second later, a new pop sounded.

The locking mechanism blew out as Kace shot at it, and he yanked the door open. "In, in, in!"

My body felt numb with fear as I darted toward the door, my arm still wrapped around Misael. As soon as we were inside, he stepped away from me, not letting me carry any more of his weight.

"I'm okay," he gritted out.

I wanted to argue. To run my hands over him and make *sure* he was okay. Blood was dripping down his arm, so how the fuck could he possibly be alright?

But before I could do any of that, Kace and Bishop were behind us, and we were running again, slipping deeper into the building. It was some kind of office building, from the small glimpses I got as we hurtled down the hall. The door Kace had shot out burst open behind us, and three big men charged in after us.

"Fuck!"

Bishop grabbed my arm and yanked me sideways as gunfire exploded behind us again. He threw all his weight against a closed office door, and it burst inward. We tumbled inside, and he twisted his body as we fell, absorbing the impact as we hit the ground. He rolled us over and leapt up, calling out to Misael, "Keep her safe!"

"On it," Misael said grimly, hauling me to my feet and wrapping his good arm around me as he pulled me toward a corner of the room. It was some kind of conference room, with a large table and chairs in the middle and an ancient TV on a rolling stand set against one wall.

Bishop and Misael stationed themselves at the door as Misael dug into his pocket and pulled out his phone. My heart beat almost as loud as the gunshots that sounded in the small space, and I couldn't seem to get my breathing under control. How many bullets did Kace and Bishop have? I didn't know much about guns, but I knew that even if they'd grabbed backup ammo from the car, they would run out eventually. And when they did, those guns in their hands would be no more useful than fucking paperweights.

"Dammit!" Misael snarled as he held the phone up to his ear. "I can't get through to Nathaniel. Motherfucker."

He cursed again, then lowered the phone and tapped on the screen quickly. He'd positioned his body in front of mine, as if wanting to make sure that anybody who made it through the door would shoot him first. His left arm still hung at his side, droplets of blood sliding off his fingers in a steady *drip, drip, drip.*

"Backup might be a fuckin' while," he called to the other two, and I saw Bish turn his head to look at Kace.

The two of them were braced on either side of the doorway, trading shots to keep the men outside at bay. I was pretty sure they'd hit at least one guy, but I wasn't positive. How many were there? Just the three who I'd seen burst into the building? More? Everything after they had t-boned Bishop's car had seemed like a blur, as if I were watching seven movies at once and trying to follow each of them.

"I'm almost out," Bishop murmured to Kace, his voice strained. "You?"

"Same," Kace grunted.

My stomach clenched, heaving as if it was trying to force its way out of my body through my throat as Misael turned to me, pulling a butterfly knife from his pocket. He flipped it open one-handed, then grimaced as he forced his injured arm to move, grabbing onto the full material of my gown's skirt.

"I'm gonna cut this off, Princess," he muttered quickly. "Make sure you can move. They're gonna get in here any second, and you need to be able to run."

I nodded, the movement jerky, but he was already following through on his words, grabbing bloody handfuls of my dress and slicing through the fabric at mid-thigh. As soon as the fabric fell away, he kissed me—just once, hard and fast, like a goodbye—then turned around again, keeping his knife out and ready.

Bishop fired once more into the hallway, and there was a grunt and a thud, but whoever he'd hit, it hadn't been enough to stop the attack. Two men rushed into the room, and shots fired wildly as Kace and Bishop grappled with them. I took a step forward without even realizing I was moving, desperate to help them somehow, but Misael's arm was like an iron bar, pressing me back.

When a third man rushed into the room, his gaze landed right on Misael. He raised his weapon to shoot, and Misael shoved me to the side as the bullet slammed into the wall where we'd been standing. I sprawled ungracefully across the floor, but Misael regained his balance quicker, sprinting toward the man and slashing out with his knife. He caught the man's arm, and our attacker gave a pained grunt. Across the room, Bishop slammed one of the other men into the rolling TV stand, still grappling for control of the weapon.

I struggled to my feet as the guy Misael had cut charged toward him, tackling Misael and taking him down. The knife fell as they landed, skittering wildly across the floor toward where Kace was locked in a fight with our third attacker.

Fuck.

Oh, fuck.

Misael was weaponless, pinned beneath the man with the gun.

My brain was screeching in panic, completely useless, but my body moved anyway. I scrambled to my feet and dove for the only weapon I could get my hands on—the discarded fabric of my dress.

Holding it in both hands, I looped it around the man's neck and face and pulled with every bit of strength I had in me. I was nowhere near as strong as the burly man was, but I'd had the element of surprise on my side. He hadn't been expecting to be suddenly blinded and choked, and he reached up with one hand to pull at the fabric.

Misael didn't miss his chance.

He bashed his forehead against the man's covered face, and the scream of pain let me know he'd broken the guy's nose. Then he grabbed the gun with both hands and twisted, yanking it from the man's grip. Blood smeared the black metal of the barrel, but his hands were steady as he aimed it.

"Cora, move!"

I released my grip on the dress and hurled myself to the side as Misael squeezed the trigger. The bullet penetrated the luxurious fabric as if it were nothing but air, and red blood exploded behind the layers of the dress. The man slumped over, sticky red blood pooling around his head.

Misael's wide eyes landed on me, and he shoved the man off him and scrambled up. His gaze tracked around the room quickly, and he called out, "Kace!"

The blond boy was locked in a battle with a man almost as vicious and brutal as he was, and my stomach churned at the sight of blood seeping from the corner of his mouth. His attention flicked to Misael, and then he kicked the man hard in the stomach, driving him back a step. Misael fired twice, and the man went down.

Not even waiting to see if the guy was dead, Kace stalked over to where Bishop was fighting the third man, swinging his fist like a wrecking ball and hitting the back of the man's head. He went down, and Bish and Kace were on him immediately.

"Here, Coralee." Misael thrust the gun into my hand. "Go help them. I'll make sure that motherfucker's dead."

He jerked his head toward the man he'd just shot, then shuffled over to him, stooping to pick up his knife as he neared the prone body. My hands shook as I held the blood-slicked gun in a tight grip, my finger brushing over the trigger. When I approached Kace and Bishop, they had the third man on his back. He looked like he was holding onto consciousness by a thread, and when I got a good look at his face, my heart stopped.

"Eli?"

It was the kid who had transferred in to Slateview High last semester. The one who had taunted me and challenged the Lost Boys. The one who worked for—

"Luke fucking Carmine."

Bishop bit out the words, his expression settling into an angry mask. He knelt next to Eli, grabbing the front of his shirt and shaking him. Eli's eyes opened, fury flashing in their depths.

"What the fuck does Luke Carmine want with us? Why does he want us dead?" Bishop demanded.

"He doesn't," Eli spat, his gaze sliding over all of us as he seemed to become more alert. "But someone does. Someone paid him for a job, and we were just carrying it out." He jerked his chin toward me. "She wasn't supposed to be part of it though."

"What?"

My skin chilled. I felt Misael come up beside me, felt him try to take the gun from me, but my frozen fingers refused to unlock. I couldn't tear my gaze away from Eli.

"What are you talking about?" I repeated, my voice a rasp.

"We were paid to take out these three fuckers," Eli grunted, sneering at me. "You weren't part of the bargain. Why would the guy want to kill his own daughter?"

TWENTY

ALL THE OXYGEN seemed to leave the room in a rush, leaving the air too thin.

What?

His... daughter?

The man who had negotiated with Luke Carmine to have the Lost Boys killed was my father.

Nausea made my stomach clench hard as dozens of thoughts raced through my head so fast it felt like I might pass out. My legs shook, and I couldn't stop staring at Eli's bloodied face as I absorbed the full weight of his words.

So many things made sense now. This was why my father had stopped trying to prevent me from seeing them, why he hadn't grounded me again even though he had known I was sneaking across town instead of going to prom committee meetings. He hadn't worried about their presence in my life

because he had been making his own arrangements to end it
—permanently.

As if killing the three boys I loved would've made me
more amenable to the idea of the arranged marriage he was
forcing on me.

Anger choked off my breath, and I could barely see
through the haze that seemed to float in my vision.

"Why the fuck would Luke take that job?" Kace asked,
his voice hard. "Going after Nathaniel's people would spark a
war, no matter who paid him to do it. Why the fuck would he
take that risk?"

"He doesn't consider it a risk anymore." Eli grinned. He'd
obviously realized he wasn't going to live through this, so he'd
decided to taunt us before the end, to lord whatever scraps of
power over us he still could. "He's been itchin' for a fight for a
long time, and he's ready now. He's sick of Nathaniel thinkin'
he owns this damn town."

"Motherfuck—"

Before Kace could finish the word, Eli moved. And I
realized that I'd been wrong. He hadn't expected to die
tonight. He'd just been biding his time, waiting for the shock
of his words to break our guard down.

His hand swept up, reaching for the gun that was still
clutched in my grip. I felt all three of the Lost Boys start to
move, felt Eli's fingers close around the barrel.

I felt my own finger squeeze the trigger, a movement so
small it barely took any effort.

Then the gun fired, and the recoil lanced up my arm like

I'd been hit with a baseball bat. I staggered, and Misael caught me as Kace stood and pulled the gun from my hand.

The room fell into silence, and Kace put his body in front of mine, cutting off my line of sight to the boy on the floor—but not in time to stop me from seeing the bullet wound in his chest.

The one I'd put there.

A rush of emotions flooded me, and my knees buckled. Misael caught me with his good arm, but the two of us almost went down before Kace pulled me into his grip. Bishop was by my side a second later, and all three boys surrounded me completely, cutting off the outside world. All the pain, death, and ugliness that surrounded us faded a little as their warmth enveloped me.

"He's gone, Princess," Bishop murmured, stroking my hair. "Don't look. You don't have to look."

"He woulda killed us if he'd gotten the chance." Kace's voice was hard as steel. "Killed *you*. You did good, Coralee. You did what you had to."

Misael didn't speak, but I could feel the warmth of his breath on my skin. I knew all three boys were sad and angry that I'd been the one to kill Eli. Not angry *at* me, but *for* me. They had tried to shield me from this part of their lives for so long, and tonight, I'd been dragged by the hair into the thick of it. Into the worst and most horrifying parts of it.

And the person who had dragged me there was my own father.

Those fucking notes I'd found on his computer made

perfect sense now. Luke Carmine must've been selling his services to both Abraham Shaw and my dad, making arrangements with whoever paid him the most, playing the two men off each other for his own benefit.

My dad had been in contact with Luke before he'd gone to prison, and apparently, he'd blamed Abraham Shaw for his incarceration, not Luke Carmine himself. Or he had decided to overlook that when he needed Luke's services again.

I clung to my three boys as thoughts crashed around in my head.

God, how could my dad be so stupid? How could he trust Luke to carry out a job for him after the man had orchestrated his arrest? Although at the moment, killing the Lost Boys seemed to align with Luke's interests, if what Eli had said was right. So I supposed, in a way, that did make Luke trustworthy, at least for my father's purposes.

He tried to have them killed.

Murdered.

Those words kept echoing in my mind, set off by the tangy, coppery scent of blood that filled the room.

Shock was only really setting in now, and instead of feeling more calm, my panic seemed to grow exponentially with every breath. But I fought it back as Bishop ran a thumb over my cheek.

"We gotta go, Coralee." He shifted his gaze to the other two, his expression hardening into that of a soldier at war. "When this team doesn't report back, they could send someone else after us. We need to get the fuck outta here before their backup arrives."

"Yeah." Misael nodded, then grimaced as they all stepped back from me a little.

I turned to him, my panic finding somewhere to land as I stared at his blood-smeared arm. "Fuck, Misael. You need a doctor. Your arm—"

"—is fine," he finished, shaking his head. "The bullet hit my shoulder, but I can still use the arm, so it didn't hit anything that important." He gave a lopsided grin that was half grimace. "I just need to wrap it up tight, stop the bleeding. That'll do for now. Bish is right. We gotta get someplace safe."

As if summoned by his words, a sound echoed into the room from out in the hallway. All four of us stiffened, and Kace raised the gun he'd taken from me, moving toward the door as quietly as a cat.

"Misael?" a voice called.

I recognized it. He obviously did too, because he gave Kace a *stand down* motion. The broad-shouldered boy was already lowering his weapon though, and a second later, Misael raised his voice and called back.

"We're in here! It's clear."

The noises in the hallway grew louder—the new arrivals no longer trying to dampen the sounds of their footsteps or hide their numbers. And it was a pretty big number, by the sound of it.

Claudio Vega stepped into the room, flanked by half a

dozen men. His gaze took in the scene at a glance, and then he crossed quickly to Misael.

"What the fuck happened here? I got your text."

"Ambush," Misael said simply. "Luke Carmine."

Claudio's eyes widened, then narrowed. He swept the room again, seeming to take in every detail this time.

"Why the fuck would he do that?" he muttered.

"He was paid." My voice didn't shake, although it sounded thin to my ears. "By my father."

Every time I said it, I believed it a little bit more. When Eli had told us that, there had been a part of my mind that had instantly rebelled at the idea. A part of my mind that *still*, despite every available piece of evidence to the contrary, hoped my father would turn out to be redeemable. But the honest truth was, some people would never change.

They would never stop manipulating, lying, or abusing their power.

My father could be a kind and reasonable man. Or at least, he could *seem* that way, as long as he got what he wanted. But wasn't that what a bully was? Someone who acted generous and magnanimous as long as no one crossed them or got in their way?

But I had dared to deny my father what he wanted.

The Lost Boys had dared to exist, to be loved by me.

And my father had set out to make us all pay for that.

Claudio's eyes widened, and he gave a low grunt that I couldn't quite interpret. Then he shook his head, seeming to compartmentalize his reaction to the news, and focused in on Misael.

"You shot?"

"Yeah." Misael shrugged his good shoulder. "Not bad though."

The look that passed over Claudio's face was the most fatherly expression I'd ever seen him wear. Worry mixed with a fierce sort of pride.

"Come on. We'll go back to the club. Get you patched up." He jerked his head toward the door, then turned to the men who had come in with him. "Check our exit."

They nodded and slid silently out the door like ghosts. Bishop's phone chimed a second later, and he answered immediately, stepping away as Claudio tore a strip of fabric from one of the dead men's shirts. I helped him wrap it around Misael's injured shoulder, and even though my stomach turned at the sight of the blood smeared over his skin, I felt better doing something.

He was paler than normal, his caramel skin looking a little gray in the dim light, but his eyes were bright, and he seemed alert. Still, I was anxious to get him back to Claudio's club and the promised medical attention.

Bishop returned a second later, slipping his phone back in his pocket. "We might have to hold off on heading to the club. Nathaniel's on his way. And he's pissed as fuck."

His voice was grim, and a shiver ran down my spine, even though I doubted Nathaniel's anger was directed at any of us. I had seen him mad though, and I had no desire to see it again. He was terrifying as a vengeful god when he was furious.

"Come on, Princess."

Kace didn't even ask before tucking the gun into the waistband of his pants and sweeping me into his arms. I wrapped my own arms around his neck, letting him hold me as we all stepped out into the hallway and headed for the front entrance.

We passed two bodies in the hall, but I made an effort not to look at them. I was sure I would see the cloth covered face of the man Misael had shot and Eli's limp, lifeless form in my dreams far too often. I didn't want to add to the images that would come back to haunt me over and over.

By the time we got outside, two more cars were pulling up. My gaze shot to the crumpled frame of Bishop's car in the distance, and my stomach pitched. I held onto Kace tighter, burying my face in his chest for a moment and just trying to absorb the fact that he was still alive. That we all were.

Against all odds, we were all still here.

When I looked up again, the back of one of the sleek black sedans opened and Nathaniel Ward stepped out. I gave a little wriggle, and Kace set me down, although he kept his arms wrapped around my waist, his solid body supporting me from behind. The cracked pavement was cold, and stones dug into my feet, but I needed to stand to face Nathaniel.

The three Lost Boys all gathered around me, their protectiveness obvious as the older man strode toward us.

Bishop and Misael each stood close on either side of me, and Claudio and his men stood a little apart.

Just like Claudio had, Nathaniel took in the sight of us and seemed to process it quickly. These men thought fast and acted fast, and they didn't waste time on shock or disbelief.

"What happened?" he asked.

Bishop, Kace, Misael, and I explained everything, going into more detail than we had with Claudio. I could see Misael's father listening intently though, and I wondered for a moment if Nathaniel would stop us—if he wouldn't want to have this debrief in front of a man who wasn't part of his crew.

But he didn't interrupt once, just listened carefully as we laid out the events of the evening. His expression darkened, and when we finished, he dipped his head in a sharp nod. His gaze moved over all of us, landing on Misael last.

"You okay?"

"Yeah. Bullet clipped me, but it's not bad."

Nathaniel nodded once more. "Good. Because I think we need to pay Mr. Van Rensselaer a visit."

TWENTY-ONE

CLAUDIO AND NATHANIEL both left a few of their men behind to deal with the scene of our attack—which I was pretty sure was going to include setting fire to the building—and the rest of us piled into two cars and headed out.

I ended up between Misael and Kace in a car with Claudio, and the silence seemed to stretch so taut I feared it would kill us all when it finally snapped. But none of the men seemed bothered by it, or at least, not enough to speak.

It took us nearly twenty minutes to reach my neighborhood, and as the car rolled smoothly down the wide, manicured streets, I ran my hands over what was left of my dress, smoothing out the skirt. The blue fabric was stained with blood and grime, and my knees were scraped and bruised. I had no idea what the rest of me looked like, but I knew that my half-assed updo had completely fallen out. A few pins still clung to my hair, and I ran my fingers through the tangled locks to pull them out, probably smearing blood in my hair in the process.

My heart beat harder and faster the closer we got to my parents' mansion, and I felt both Misael and Kace reach for me, each resting a hand on my knee. I hadn't asked what Nathaniel planned to do with my father, and I realized in retrospect that I should have—not that I had the power to change his mind, whatever he'd decided.

But a wave of nausea roiled my stomach as I wondered if the crime lord planned to kill my father.

That was the way of the world I had found myself a part of, after all. In this world, you killed your enemies before they killed you. And if someone made an attempt on your life and failed, you took them out before they could try again.

"It'll be okay, Coralee. We'll keep you safe," Kace muttered, so quietly I could barely hear him. I glanced toward the front seat, wondering if he hadn't wanted Claudio to hear.

God, was I about to find myself in the middle of a *second* shootout tonight? What if Nathaniel decided I deserved punishment just like my father?

The Lost Boys wouldn't let him harm me.

They'd die trying to protect me.

Goose bumps broke out over my skin, a riot of nerves making my blood prickle inside my veins. This night was a long fucking way from over.

When we pulled up outside the house, I gave Claudio's driver the code to open the gate, and it swung open on silent hinges. The two cars rolled to a stop in the driveway, and we all piled out. Misael had wiped most of the blood off his hand, and the bandage on his shoulder was keeping more blood from dripping down his arm, but we all looked like shit. Kace had a cut across his cheek and a gash in the front of his shirt, and I was still barefoot, shivering in the cold night air.

Nathaniel, Bishop, and two other men stepped out of the car ahead of us, and we all headed up the front steps. It was late, almost midnight, but the lights were still on in parts of the house. I wondered if Dad was waiting up for confirmation that his hit had been carried out, and my stomach twisted so violently at the thought that I almost hurled into the perfectly manicured hedges that bordered the steps on either side.

I half expected Nathaniel to shoot out the lock like Kace had back at the office building. But instead, he looked to me. "Do you have a key?"

The question caught me so off guard that I blinked at him like an idiot for several seconds. *A key.* It was so... so *normal.* So bland.

But of course, it made perfect sense. Nathaniel was wealthy and well-connected in Baltimore's underground, but just because he'd managed to avoid getting busted for his criminal activity so far didn't mean he was above the law. Why bother kicking in the door or shooting out the lock when it could trigger an alarm? Especially if he had a way in that didn't require any of that.

"Um, yeah," I stammered.

I hadn't wanted to bring a purse to the dance, so I'd stuck

my key in my bra. Cheeks flaming, I reached my hand down the front of my dress and fished around, trying to avoid making eye contact with anyone. All three of the Lost Boys seemed to puff up a little bit, glaring at the others as if daring any of them to take a peek.

Fortunately, none of the men with us were idiots or pervs, so no one ogled me as I drew the key out of my cleavage. I handed it to Nathaniel, and he gave me an almost gentlemanly nod before he took it and turned to unlock the door.

We all stepped inside, moving quietly, and my heart kicked against my ribs as I realized just how many of the men around me had weapons drawn. Both of Nathaniel's guys did, and Kace had pulled his stolen gun from the waistband of his pants. Claudio held a gun too, and from the look on his face, I could guess whether he hoped to use it tonight or not.

Nathaniel took the lead as we headed toward the light spilling into the foyer from a room down the hall. I knew it was coming from Dad's office, and my legs wobbled with every step, my head buzzing like it was full of bees.

I could try to break free from the group and run to him, try to warn him what was coming. Or I could shout the warning from here. Give him a few precious seconds to flee or prepare a defense.

I *could*.

There were so many things I could do.

But all I did was keep walking forward, my bare feet more silent than anyone else's as we stalked toward Dad's office. The door wasn't closed all the way. It hung a few inches open, spilling light into the hallway. I could hear the light tapping of fingers on a keyboard inside, but the sound stopped abruptly when Nathaniel pushed open the door and stepped inside.

The rest of us followed, and I entered the room in time to see Dad shoot to his feet, a look of panic and anger on his face.

"What the f—"

He broke off when he caught sight of me, and the double take he did was almost comical. I might've laughed out loud if I didn't still feel like I was about to barf. The sight he must be taking in was only funny in the darkest, most macabre sense of the word.

His daughter, her hair and face smeared with blood and dirt, her knees scraped, her skin bruised.

Wearing half a prom dress.

He gawped at me for a second, looking truly taken aback by something for the first time since the night the Feds had come to arrest him.

"C-Cordelia?" he stammered.

At the sound of my name on my father's lips, all three of the Lost Boys tensed, as if my dad might be able to hurt me with that word alone. The slight movement of their bodies drew his attention, and I saw his expression darken as he took them in.

In the warm, buttery light of the lamps in his study, our wounds actually looked worse, not better—as if the contrast between our luxurious surroundings and our battered bodies only highlighted how gruesome we all looked.

"Hi, Dad."

It was all I could force past my lips, and I truly didn't know if the words were a greeting or a goodbye.

Why wasn't I trying to stop this? Why wasn't I putting myself in between him and the men who had invaded his home?

Because he doesn't deserve it.

He doesn't deserve my sacrifice.

The time in my life when I might've been willing to give my life to save my father's was done. I wouldn't pull the trigger myself, but the man in front of me felt so little like a father anymore that the innate impulse to protect my own flesh and blood barely raised its head.

"Mr. Van Rensselaer, we have a problem."

Nathaniel's deep voice drew my father's attention, and his head snapped over to stare at the handsome, sharp-faced man. His eyes widened just enough that I was sure he knew who Nathaniel was, and I saw him register just how many guns were pointed in his direction.

This might all be captured on his security cameras, but that wouldn't do him much good later if he died right now.

Slowly, Dad raised his hands in the air, holding them out in front of him in a defensive gesture. "I don't know what you're talking about."

"Don't you?" The way the words fell from Nathaniel's lips, they hardly sounded like a question.

"No, I—"

"Do you recognize these three men?"

Nathaniel gestured to the Lost Boys beside me. It struck me suddenly that he'd called them men, not boys, and when I glanced around at all three of them, I realized that's exactly what they were. They had always been powerful and dominating, but as they stared down my father with cold hatred in their eyes, they looked every bit the grown men they were. There was nothing boyish left in their features, just pure masculinity.

"I—" My father broke off, clearing his throat slightly. Probably trying to buy himself time to decide whether to lie or not. But the way Nathaniel was posing the questions made it clear he already knew the answers, and Dad must've realized lying would be a quick way to lose this game.

He nodded, thrusting his chin out slightly in an expression I'd seen him wear dozens of times. Imperious confidence.

"Yes. I do know them. They tried to steal what belongs to me."

A low growl rumbled in Kace's throat, and I suddenly really wished he wasn't the one holding the gun. Not for my dad's sake, but for his. I didn't want him to walk out of here with more blood on his hands, but a few more comments like that from my father, and I knew he'd have a hard time holding back.

"So you tried to have them killed? Is that right?" Nathaniel's voice was still calm and even, almost bland, and when Dad didn't answer after a few long beats, he continued anyway. "You put out a hit on three of my men tonight. As I said, that means we have a problem."

Dad's face paled slightly, a muscle in his jaw clenching. "They tried to steal my daughter! She's *engaged*. I've made arrangements. I will not let three pieces of shit off the street drag her away from that."

Ignoring that tirade entirely, Nathaniel raised his gun, leveling it at my father's head. "I'm only going to say this once. Nothing gives you the right to come after me or my men. Have you forgotten what you owe me?"

My heart slammed against my ribs as I watched my father's proud expression dim slightly. Yeah, he remembered. How could he fucking forget? No matter what Dad might claim about having had it under control, Nathaniel was the reason he was out of prison. The reason he was a free man.

Free to make deals with a devil named Luke Carmine.

Free to try to kill the men I loved.

He doesn't deserve to be free.

"I could deal with this right now, in the manner most befitting an attempt on their lives," Nathaniel went on, his finger tightening almost imperceptibly on the trigger. "An eye for an eye."

My breath caught in my throat, and my heart felt like it was pumping so hard it might explode. A small trickle of sweat worked its way down Dad's face, glinting in the lamp light.

"But..." The crime lord uncurled his finger, cocking his

head to the side slightly. "...perhaps there are better solutions to be found. You did all this because you want your daughter to be married so badly?"

It seemed to take Dad a moment to find his voice, and when he did, it was rough and scratchy. "Yes. The marriage will ensure security for both her and her family."

Nathaniel considered that for a moment, his head swiveling left and right as he took in all of us lined up alongside him. Then he turned back to my father and nodded.

"Alright. She'll get married."

TWENTY-TWO

IT FELT like the floor had dropped out from under me.

Like I was free falling through space.

Like I would fall and fall forever.

The world tilted in my periphery as I fought to keep my legs under me, turning to stare at Nathaniel with wide eyes and my mouth hanging half open.

What?

What the actual fuck?

On the drive over here, my overactive brain had gone through dozens of worst-case scenarios, up to and including the one where gunfire erupted and we all died.

But I had never imagined this.

After everything, after all that had happened, Nathaniel was going to let my dad go through with his plan? What, would he agree to let Dad marry me off to Barrett in exchange for a promise to never attack the Lost Boys again?

Before I could react or say anything, Nathaniel turned to Claudio. "A marriage connection to the Van Rensselaer family could be very beneficial. You asked what our partnership would be worth. I can offer you this."

Claudio blinked, looking startled. "Marriage? I have no interest in marrying—"

"Not you." Nathaniel shook his head, then shifted his gaze to Misael before looking back at Claudio. "Your son."

My father made a noise that was somewhere between a scoff and a squawk. "What? I just told you I have no interest in letting her associate with trash like him! I will not—"

He didn't get the finish his tirade. Claudio was across the room in three long strides, grabbing Dad by the thick, shiny hair he was so proud of and jamming the barrel of the gun under his chin.

"Call my son trash one more time."

Claudio's voice vibrated with fury, and a spark of something warm flashed in my chest. His response to defend his son had been instantaneous, and unlike Nathaniel, he wasn't playing it cool and collected. It occurred to me that I should be more terrified that this man would shoot my father, and I searched inside my heart for the feelings I knew I should have, but I couldn't find them.

Maybe the accumulated weight of everything I'd been through tonight was muffling my emotions, making it hard to process them. Too much had happened too fast for my brain to keep up with it all.

I had killed a man tonight.

I had let a group of dangerous criminals into my house to threaten my father.

I had been offered up in marriage to one of them.

That last thought stuck in the front of my mind, and even as I watched my father's eyes go wide with fear, I repeated it over and over in my head.

Married.

Married.

Married.

But not to Barrett King. To Misael Alviar.

Claudio kept his grip on my father as he glanced over at Nathaniel. "You really think I want this fucker as my in-law?"

Nathaniel smiled. "I don't expect you'll be having many Sunday brunches together. But I think he could be a valuable asset."

I could see my father twitch, as if he wanted to protest but knew better than to actually do it.

A valuable asset. That was what Dad had tried to turn me into by marrying me off to Barrett. Apparently, now that the tables were turned, he didn't like how that shoe fit at all.

Claudio considered that silently for a moment. Then he finally released Dad, stepping back but keeping his weapon raised. He glanced over at Misael, who stood silent beside me. "Is this what you want?"

Misael's body jerked slightly. He still looked a little ashen from blood loss, and I had a feeling he might be as shell-shocked from the emotional whiplash of the evening as I was.

Instead of answering his father, he turned to look at me, his dark eyes intense and earnest. His gaze flicked up to the two boys on my other side, and I could see an almost tortured expression cross his face.

"Can we have a moment?" I asked quickly, angling my head to catch Nathaniel's gaze. "Will you watch my dad?"

He nodded, understanding in his eyes. "Of course."

Not bothering to respond to the outraged sound my father made, I grabbed the boys who stood beside me and hustled them outside. Moving quickly, I pulled them toward the sitting room down the hall, wondering if Mom was asleep upstairs, still utterly clueless about what was happening in the rooms below her. She'd be in for an unpleasant as fuck shock tomorrow.

As soon as we stepped into the sitting room, I flicked on the light. None of us sat—I was so wired I could barely stand still—and Misael and I turned to each other and spoke at the same moment.

"You don't have to do this," we both said.

I blinked, staring at him in surprise as I heard my words echoed back to me.

"Do you... not want to?" I asked slowly.

He licked his lips, opening his mouth and closing it once before shaking his head and trying again.

"Coralee, if we got married, you would be *in* this life. Not just around it. A part of it. Forever. That's how this shit works. Once you're in, you don't get out. Especially not if you're bound by marriage. I can't fuckin' ask you to do that.

And besides, what about the shit with my dad and my mom? She almost got killed because of him. I told you I won't let that happen to you, and I meant it. I can't—"

"Misael." I held up a hand, viscerally aware of all three of the men around me, feeling the heat of Kace and Bishop's bodies as they stood close to me on either side. "You didn't answer my question. Do *you* not want to marry me?"

His expression shifted, and I swore I could see his heart in his eyes.

His soul.

Everything about him that made him sweet and funny and protective and dangerous. It was all laid bare in the beautiful brown depths of his irises.

"Cora, I'd fuckin' marry you tomorrow if I could. I love you."

Tension I hadn't even realized I had been holding in my body since the fight with Luke Carmine's men—hell, probably since long before that—melted from my muscles, leaving me feeling lighter and more free than I'd felt in a long time.

Staring into Misael's eyes, I realized that I didn't have a single doubt. Not one. Not about his feelings for me, or mine for him. Not about my willingness to join the life he was destined to lead, to be a part of it forever.

I'd had plenty of time to think about what becoming part of the Lost Boys' world would mean.

And I wanted that.

I wanted to be part of a world where people fought

fiercely, but they loved fiercely too. Where I could be the person I had slowly been discovering inside myself these past several months. Where I could be with the three men who'd claimed my soul.

My hands found Kace's and Bishop's, gripping them tight, and I turned to look at the two boys on either side of me. "Would you be okay with this? It wouldn't mean I love either of you less. I wouldn't want it to change anything between us."

Bishop reached up to run a knuckle down my cheek, ignoring the dried blood and dirt smeared over the back of his hand. His hazel eyes were impossible to read as he stared down at me.

"Fuck, Princess," he said after a moment. "Everything Misael just said is true. We *shouldn't* want this. By rights, we should make sure you stay as far away from us as possible." At the look of panic that flared in my eyes, he caught my chin and leaned down to kiss me roughly. When he pulled back, a small smile curved his lips. "But I think we all know by now that's never gonna fuckin' happen. You're ours. We're yours. And we'll burn down the whole world to protect you if we have to, but we're not letting you go."

"Even if I can only marry one of you?" I asked softly, my heart swelling in my chest.

"Will you love me less?"

"No!"

The word burst out of me, and Bishop's smile stretched wider.

"Then I don't give a fuck whose ring you wear." Something in his expression shifted, a sort of possessiveness I'd never seen before. He shifted his grip on my hand, pressing my palm to my stomach with his larger one covering mine. "Besides, the thought of you pregnant with one of our babies? Of your belly round and beautiful with one of our little ones. Fuck."

The last word came out as a groan, and he pressed his lips to mine as if he wanted to get started on making that happen right now.

My core clenched, and my stomach fluttered with excitement and nerves. I had always known I wanted children, but it'd been a vague wish, a dim idea with hazy details. But now, I could see it as clearly in my mind's eye as anything tangible and real.

A little boy or girl with Bishop's angular features, Misael's caramel skin, or Kace's moss-green eyes.

A baby that we would all love.

A child who would grow up more protected and cherished than any of us had.

When Bishop and I broke apart, I bit my lip, tasting him on my swollen, tingling skin. I nodded, and his smile grew impossibly wider. Then I turned to Kace, intent on getting an answer out of him too. I wouldn't do this if any of the Lost Boys were opposed to it. I wouldn't let something like this drive us apart.

But before I could pose the question to him, he hauled me into his arms and kissed me the same way he had back in the nurse's office at Highland Park Academy. It was a kiss that said more than words ever could. A kiss that contained volumes.

But the one word it spoke louder than anything else was *yes*.

My hands clutched at his shoulders, and I felt Bishop and Misael close ranks around us as I drowned in Kace's lips. Hands moved over me as three warm bodies surrounded me, and the truth of what this decision meant finally began to sink in.

I got to keep this.

I would never lose this.

The Lost Boys were mine.

Fully and completely mine.

NOW THAT WE'D made our decision, all I wanted to do was bask in it, to ignore the rest of the world and spend a week wrapped up in three strong pairs of arms.

But unfortunately, the real world refused to be put off.

After spending a few more minutes talking in low voices, the four of us headed back to my dad's office, a united force with me at the center. The moment we stepped inside, I was sure everyone present knew what the answer would be. My father's face stiffened, a look of anger and betrayal passing over his features. Claudio looked thoughtful, and Nathaniel seemed deeply pleased.

"It's what we want," Misael said seriously, his fingers tangling with mine as he spoke. "I want to marry Cora."

"And I want to marry Misael," I echoed, butterflies flapping wildly in my stomach.

"Good." Nathaniel beamed. "It's settled then." He shot a glance at my father. "We'll draw up the arrangements, and this will satisfy the favor you owe me. You will not cut Cora off as your heir or disavow her in any way, and you will not attempt to take the lives of her new husband or *any* of my men."

My father's nostrils flared, and his gaze shifted from Nathaniel to Claudio and back before he nodded. He might be a stubborn, heartless, and demanding man, but he wasn't a stupid one. He'd clearly realized that he was out-matched and out-gunned. By tying my family to Claudio's, Nathaniel had effectively cut him off from buying any more help from Luke Carmine. Luke would see my father as an enemy now, possibly even a traitor, and he wouldn't lift a finger to help him.

A flicker of something like sympathy rose in my heart.

In a way, I was using my dad the same way he'd been planning to use me. My wedding to Barrett would've been a political and economic arrangement, a business deal. I would've been stuck in a loveless, awful marriage for the rest of my life just so my father could benefit from it. But now, with my planned marriage to Misael, the tables were turned. The connections gained by this union wouldn't benefit my dad at all. They would benefit Claudio and Misael, and by extension, me.

I could see Dad struggling against the inevitability of this, searching desperately for a way out of it like an animal in a cage. But there *was* no way out—no better option. He had been slowly painting himself into this corner ever since he had first contacted Luke Carmine, ever since he and Abraham Shaw had begun their game of betrayal and deceit. Everything my father had done was finally catching up to him, and as I considered that, the flame of sympathy in my chest sputtered out.

He would live.

He would survive like he always did.

But he would no longer have any power over me.

And I wasn't even a little sorry about that.

TWENTY-THREE

IF I THOUGHT the event planner my dad had hired to make arrangements for the wedding in July had been moving fast, well... that was nothing compared to how fast things moved after I agreed to marry Misael.

Nathaniel sent me and the Lost Boys upstairs to pack a bag, and it was agreed that I would stay with him and Josephine until after the wedding. I would've protested that I wanted to live with my boys, but since the wedding was planned for just one week away, I decided not to raise a fuss. Claudio was already making plans to secure us a house in a part of Baltimore where a lot of his crew lived, and I had a feeling he would have it all taken care of in just a few days.

Kace, Misael, and Bishop moved around my room silently as they helped me pack, and when I had everything I needed for the moment, they carried my bags down the hall. I hesitated at the top of the stairs, gazing down the hallway in the direction of my parents' bedroom. Should I go wake my mom and tell her goodbye?

The thought died almost as soon as it arose. It was so late it was early, and my adrenaline had spiked and ebbed so many times tonight that I felt like the walking dead. I didn't have it in me to deal with whatever my mother's reaction would be. And besides, I would see her at the wedding—if she chose to come.

When we returned to the study, I was relieved to find that the guns had all been lowered. Not that I expected my father and Claudio to get along at all, but it would be awkward to have weapons drawn as I said my vows. My father still looked angry and bitter, but he made no further protest as all of us headed for the door. He followed behind us, and although his bearing was still stiff and imperious, he looked... smaller somehow. As if his almost inhuman seeming power had been diminished in my eyes.

He was wealthy and domineering, but at the end of the day, he was just a man.

And he had lost this game.

I turned to him as everyone began to file out the front door into the cool darkness outside.

"It didn't have to be this way, Dad. I wanted to love you. All my life, I've wanted to love you. I've wanted you to be worthy of it. But I can't wait any longer for you to show a side of yourself that doesn't exist."

His brows lowered, a muscle in his jaw jumping. "You

are my daughter in name only from now on, Cordelia. What you've done is unforgivable."

I shook my head. That would've hurt me once, but now it just made me smile sadly. "I don't need your forgiveness. And I don't need your love. It took me eighteen years to realize that."

Bishop's arm wrapped around my shoulders, solid and comforting, and the other two boys fell into place around me as we walked out of the house and down the front steps.

Leaving my old life behind for good.

THE HEAVY THUMP of dance music vibrated through my whole body as we made our way through the club. Spotlight was as packed with sweaty, gyrating bodies as it had been the first time we'd come here, and a smile tugged at my lips as I remembered that evening.

It'd been three days since my ill-fated prom night, and I could still feel the lingering effects of that night everywhere in my body. My bruises had settled into dark purple marks, and the scratches and scrapes that decorated my body had scabbed over.

The boys were still beat to shit too, but they were healing up as well. Misael had gotten the wound in his shoulder stitched up, and although he still favored that arm, he could use it if he was careful.

More than my lingering injuries, it was my mind and heart that felt the brunt of the events of prom night. Although I felt safe at Nathaniel's house, I still had a hard time sleeping peacefully. Images of prone bodies with blood seeping from them filled my nightmares, and Eli's face appeared in my dreams frequently. I had hated him when he'd been alive, and I knew he would've killed us if he'd gotten the gun from me. But that didn't make it any easier to process the fact that I had been the one to kill him.

I understood much more of what Kace had gone through in the aftermath of Flint's death, and the blond boy had been the one to hold me while I cried when everything finally hit me the night after prom. He had sat with me for what must've been hours in my borrowed room at Nathaniel's house, not even speaking, just offering me the comfort of his presence and his *understanding*.

In a striking contrast to the trauma that still haunted me, wedding plans were well underway. I had assumed it would be a pretty simple affair, maybe even just a courthouse wedding. But apparently, the pomp and circumstance mattered as much as the marriage certificate itself, because it was shaping up to be lavish and well-attended. Josephine was handling a lot of the details, working with Claudio's people and asking my input on things without overloading me with minutia.

It made sense, in a way.

This was a symbolic tying together of families, and Claudio and Nathaniel both wanted their people to be well aware of what this meant. The two men had formed a full alliance, and this wedding was a gift from Nathaniel to Claudio.

Their first order of business as a combined force would be to deal with Luke Carmine—and that was what had brought me and my men to the club tonight.

Just like he had the first time we'd come to visit Muse, Kace led us to the back of the club into a red-walled room filled with black leather furniture.

The man waiting for us grinned when we stepped inside, gesturing for us to sit down.

"My friends. Good to see you again."

Muse was tall and lanky, and he had a cat-like way of moving that made him seem both relaxed and predatory. Long black dreadlocks woven through with gold accents spilled over his dark shoulders, and he wore a tank top that molded to his muscled chest. His leather pants gleamed in the dim light as he crossed his booted feet, leaning back in his seat as he dipped his chin in greeting.

"Muse."

Bishop returned his nod, and the man gestured for us all to sit. As we settled onto a couch opposite him, his gaze landed on me.

"Cora Van Rensselaer. I've been hearin' your name pop up all over town lately. Guess congratulations are in order."

I flushed slightly. "Thank you."

He cocked an eyebrow, his dark eyes studying me. "And I presume you ain't here just to tell me you're gettin' married. I already know all about that, darlin'."

"No." I shook my head, scooting forward on the seat. The three men around me let me take the lead, and I appreciated their silent show of support. "I have some other information I think you'll want. Something I hope will repay the debt I owe you."

Muse didn't lean forward, but I could see his gaze sharpen. He was interested. Intrigued. Cocking his head to one side, he spread both arms over the back of the couch. "Anxious to get outta this deal before you become a married woman, aye?"

I felt the Lost Boys shift around me at that, but I put a hand on Misael's knee to calm him.

In actual fact, that was a huge part of the reason we'd come here now. With my upcoming wedding into Claudio Vega's family and operation, not to mention a union that would bring me even closer into Nathaniel Ward's fold, I couldn't afford to be beholden to anyone outside their organization—not even someone as generally neutral as Muse, a man who peddled in information and rarely took sides.

But there was no reason to outright admit that to him.

"I'm here because I think what I know is worth at least as much as the information you gave me last time we visited," I said calmly, and Muse's gaze narrowed as he assessed me.

Finally, he nodded. "Alright. Let's hear it, then."

"You told us last time that all roads to my father's arrest led to Luke Carmine. And you were right. But it's more than that." I met his gaze, watching him closely to gauge his reaction to my words. "He's been trying to play all sides, accepting jobs from conflicting parties and pitting them against each other. He did it to my father and Abraham Shaw, and I'm sure he's done it to others."

As I spoke, a feeling of satisfaction welled inside me. I could see the glint in Muse's eyes that told me this information was as good as I thought it was. Honor might not exist among all thieves, but I had learned during my time in this world that loyalty was prized above almost anything else.

And Luke Carmine had none.

Muse rubbed a hand over his chin, the thick rings on his fingers shining brightly. "And you've got proof of this?"

"Yes."

I glanced at Bishop, and he pulled out the emails I had printed off in my Dad's office weeks ago, handing them over to Muse.

The informant unfolded the papers and scanned them, his tongue darting out to lick his full lips. The emails I had printed were vague enough that I wasn't sure it would've convinced law enforcement to go after my dad—but for a man like Muse, who had his fingers in so many parts of Baltimore's underworld, it was only one piece of a puzzle.

And this piece had completed the picture.

His gaze snapped up to me. "This is good shit."

I smiled. "I know."

"Yeah, alright." He nodded, still scanning through the papers. "We're even. I ain't one to stiff my friends, and this is a fair trade for what I gave you."

I could feel the men beside me relax slightly. It was done. I was free. I would begin my new life with Misael and the others with no debts or bonds.

A wicked gleam entered Muse's eyes, and his gaze tracked over all of us. He grinned, revealing white teeth. "You know this is gonna cause a shitload of trouble for Luke Carmine when this gets out, aye? He'll lose allies faster than flies droppin' on a hot day."

Bishop's answering smile was fierce and feral.

"We're counting on it."

TWENTY-FOUR

"YOU LOOK LOVELY."

Josephine smiled at me as I smoothed down the skirt of my dress. I had decided on an ivory gown with a full skirt and a sweetheart neckline, nothing nearly as elaborate or expensive as the dress I was sure Mom would've picked out for me for my wedding with Barrett.

But this was more beautiful than anything she could've chosen.

Because it was me.

And it was the dress I would marry Misael Alviar in.

And that made it fucking perfect.

"Thanks, Jo." I grinned at her.

The first time I'd called her that, it'd been totally by accident, and I'd seen her head jerk back slightly in surprise. Then she had smiled, a look that was almost motherly passing over her face. I had already been close with her, but spending a week living in her house, working closely with her on wedding arrangements, had solidified the bond between us.

"Your men won't be able to take their eyes off you," she added, reaching out to tuck a trailing curl of blonde hair behind my ear. Then she pursed her lips, studying me. "Are you happy, Cora?"

"Yes." My lips were stretching wide even before I spoke, and I couldn't tamp down the rush of butterflies that filled my stomach as I thought about what today would bring. "I'm so happy. This is—it's *right*, Jo. I just know it is."

She nodded. "I know that feeling. I'm glad. Because it won't always be easy. I'm sure you already know that, with everything you've been through. There will be difficult times, and I'd be lying if I told you this life and this world isn't cruel and unforgiving sometimes. But the *rightness*? The love? That will get you through all of those times."

I bit my lip, tears burning the backs of my eyes. I did know that already, understood it on a visceral level. I wasn't expecting the world to turn into sunshine and roses just because I'd said my wedding vows.

But I didn't care.

I'd have my men with me, and together, we could face anything.

I had stopped going to classes at Highland Park the day after prom, and had been studying for the GED instead. A diploma from an elite high school wouldn't mean much in the life I was entering into, and although I definitely still planned to continue my schooling, I would be doing it for *me*, not to fit some mold my parents had built for me the day I was born. The one they had spent my entire life trying to force me to fit into.

"I really love them," I whispered. "All of them. I can't wait to do this."

She pulled me into a tight hug, then drew back to look me in the eyes. "They're lucky to have you, Cora. We all are."

I blinked rapidly a few times, determined not to cry until the actual ceremony, when I wasn't sure I'd be able to hold myself back. I was so overwhelmed with feelings that it wouldn't take much to open the floodgates.

But her words touched me deeply. They were a reminder that although this marriage was about alliances and power in some ways, it was about so much more than that in all the ways that mattered.

It was about love.

About *family*.

"I'm lucky to have you too, Jo," I murmured.

She smiled and kissed me on the cheek, then turned and slipped out the door, leaving me alone in the small room at the back of the church. It was set up as a suite where the bride could prepare and get dressed, with an ornate vanity along one wall, a full-length mirror in the corner, and a couch and several chairs in the middle of the room.

The guests would be arriving in about an hour, but I'd come early to get ready. It hadn't taken as long as I'd expected, so now I was dressed and made up, with my hair all done, and I still had time to kill.

I was about to head back toward the mirror in the corner for one more look when the door opened behind me.

Misael's dark mop of hair appeared a second later as he poked his head inside.

Maybe the prim and proper thing to do would've been to yelp and shoo him out, insisting he wasn't supposed to see me in my dress before the wedding. But I had seen far too little of my men this week with everything that had been going on. We'd be moving into our new house soon, and I couldn't wait to settle into a life with them. To wake up beside them every day, to fall asleep in their arms every night. To share meals together, to do fucking *laundry* together. To have our lives intertwined with each other's, all four of us in an unbreakable bond.

So instead of telling Misael to go, I made a beeline for him, striding quickly to the door and hauling him inside before attacking him with ravenous lips. He responded instantly, his arms coming around my waist as he delved his tongue into my mouth as if he'd been starving for me.

A chuckle from behind him made me pull away, and when I looked up, I saw Bishop and Kace standing there. Kace closed the door behind them as Bish crossed his arms over his chest, looking good enough to fucking eat in his charcoal gray suit.

I pulled away from Misael, stepping back to admire the sight of all three of them. They were each dressed in well-tailored suits, and it was the most dressed up I had ever seen them. I liked their usual look, which was casual and rough around the edges just like they were.

But this? Well, I liked this too.

"You keep fuckin' us with those pretty green eyes of yours, Princess," Bishop said, his voice both teasing and heated, "and we won't be responsible for any damage to your dress when we tear it off your body."

My nipples hardened at his words, and my core throbbed. God, that sounded fucking amazing. Well, minus the "destroying my dress" part. I'd need it when I walked down the aisle in an hour, and I wasn't letting anything stop me from marrying Misael today.

Besides, now that the men were here, I could do something I'd been wanting to do for the past few days. I just hadn't found a good time for it yet, but now seemed like the perfect opportunity.

"Hang on."

I held up a finger, then crossed to the vanity and opened the little box I had left on it, making sure to shield my actions from the men with my body. My stomach clenched with nerves as I closed my fist around the two silver bands that I'd taken from the box. I hoped Kace and Bishop would like them, and that they'd understand everything the rings represented.

The three men were watching me with curious looks when I returned to stand before them, and I glanced from Bishop to Kace, taking in their handsome features—so different from each other, but each so beautiful in their own way.

"I wanted to make sure you know that today, even though I'm marrying Misael, the bond that's being sanctified is between all four of us. I will never love one of you more than the others. I will always need all three of you." I opened my fist, revealing the two rings. "So I got you these. And my wedding band will be made of three rings too. So we'll know, and the whole world will know, that we belong to each other."

A moment of silence came at the end of my words, and I took a nervous breath as it stretched out longer and longer.

Shit. Maybe this wasn't a good idea—

The thought was forced from my mind as Kace gathered me up in a crushing hug, kissing me so deeply I almost bent over backward. I closed my hand around the rings again quickly to keep from dropping them to the floor, my empty hand clutching at Kace for balance.

When he finally stopped kissing me and brought me upright again, I was panting for breath.

"So... you like them?" I asked.

His light green eyes burned with love. "Fuck, yes."

A goofy grin spread across my face, and I slipped the rings onto both his and Bishop's fingers, my hands shaking a little as adrenaline and joy flooded me.

The instant Bishop's ring was on, he grabbed my face, his fingers threading through my hair as he kissed me with the same sort of hunger Kace just had.

I could feel the other two men close on either side of me, could feel their heat and the hardness of their cocks as they pressed up against me, and the answering fire that lit under my skin made me moan.

"I can't... mess up... my dress," I murmured in between hot kisses, saying the words but hardly even meaning them anymore. Fuck it. I'd walk down the aisle in the sweater and jeans I had worn over to the church if I had to.

"The dress doesn't have to be a part of this," Bishop growled against my lips. "But you don't get to do something like you just did and not expect to be thoroughly fucked afterward."

My body felt like it might burst into flames as his words traveled straight to my clit. Groaning, I nodded, giving in to the impulses raging inside me.

Two sets of hands fumbled with the fasteners at the back of my dress, and as soon as they reached the last one, they let the fabric fall, letting my dress pool around my feet in a billowy cloud. Bishop broke our kiss a second before Kace hefted me over his shoulder in nothing more than my bra, panties, and high heels.

I yelped when his palm cracked hard against my ass, and a flood of wetness dampened my panties a second later. His large hand massaged away the sting, making my thighs clench together, and I could hear the appreciative sounds of the other two men as Kace carried me to the couch. I did my best to stay still, but my hips were already shifting restlessly, my pelvis grinding against his chest as I sought any kind of friction against my clit.

"Greedy," he rumbled, and I *felt* the pleased sound all the way through my body. "So fucking greedy."

A second later, I was deposited on the couch. When I looked up at Kace, I saw him jerk his chin toward Bishop.

"Lock the door," he said, his voice rough.

My thighs clenched together again, and I slid a hand down my stomach, so turned on already that I was desperate for a little relief.

But Misael caught my hand before I could reach my panties, holding it in a gentle but firm grip as he peeled it away from my body. "Uh uh, Coralee. Save that for us."

As if to demonstrate his point, he pressed his lips to my mound, letting me feel the warmth of his breath through the thin fabric of my underwear. He knelt beside the couch, and as he continued to kiss my panties-covered core, the other two boys joined him. They were all on their knees in a row beside the couch, and it occurred to me that they might almost look like they were praying—except this prayer was too debauched and filthy to belong in any church.

Bishop kissed my lips again as his hands caressed my breasts, massaging away the building ache inside them. Kace's lips drifted over my legs, making parts of my body I rarely thought about explode with sensation as he nipped and licked my skin. When he reached my knee, he dragged one leg off the couch, spreading my legs wider and giving Misael access to more of me. He took it, clamping his mouth over the soaked fabric of my panties and sucking, flicking his tongue over my clit and making me arch off the couch.

"Do you want us all, Coralee?" Kace rasped, and the instant he said it, I knew exactly what he meant.

Hunger swept through me like a forest fire, and I grabbed on to Misael's head, holding him in place as my hips rose up to meet the pressure of his lips. I wrenched my mouth away from Bishop's as a throaty cry fell from my lips.

"Yes!"

Everything stopped for a moment as the three men drew back to look at me, and I blinked up at them desperately. I'd been so close to coming already, and I wanted more. So much more.

"All of you," I breathed, my chest rising and falling hard. "At the same time. Please."

They descended on me again so fast that I barely knew what happened, lips and teeth and hands moving over me with the same desperate hunger I felt. Bishop unclasped my bra as Kace and Misael worked my panties down my legs, and then I felt two of Kace's thick fingers slide inside me as Misael's tongue lapped at my clit.

And my world flew to pieces.

I bucked against their hold, the pleasure wracking my body almost too much to endure. I had kicked off my shoes somewhere in the middle of all this, and now my toes curled into the soft fabric of the couch. I panted into Bishop's mouth as he kissed me over and over again, devouring my sounds of pleasure.

When the tension finally drained from my body, I blinked, the world coming into focus around me again. All three of the men kneeling beside me stood, and I bit my lip as I watched them undress, loosening their ties and pulling them off before shrugging out of their jackets and unbuttoning their shirts.

It was like a slow unveiling, an unwrapping of three hot-as-fuck gifts, and I let out a soft whimper when they all finally shucked their boxer briefs. Misael's stitches were covered with a small white bandage, and my gaze traveled over not just the stunning display of muscle before me, but the injuries each of the men still wore.

It was a visceral reminder of how lucky we all were to still be here, to still be *alive*.

I didn't know how much more time we had before the wedding was supposed to start. I didn't know whether the guests would be able to hear sounds from this room as they filtered into the church and sat in the pews.

But I couldn't bring myself to care.

Bishop stepped up beside me, and when I sat up to kiss him, he bent to press his lips to mine. Then he wrapped his arms around me, maneuvering us so that he lay on the couch beneath me. His hard cock was sandwiched between us, and when I moved my hips, sliding my wet folds along his thick length, he grunted into my mouth.

"Are you ready, Coralee?" he murmured.

Yes.

More than ready.

It felt like my whole life had been building toward this moment, toward the sealing of a bond between me and three lost parts of myself. Parts I had known in another life, maybe, or parts my soul had claimed as its own.

I nodded, kissing him again even as I rose up onto my knees, giving myself the right angle to impale myself on his cock. As I sank down onto him, Misael and Kace traced the lines of my body with their hands, their movements following mine as I began to ride Bishop slowly, dragging out each undulation of my hips.

My arousal coated his cock and seeped from the place where he sank deep into me, and as the pleasant burn of another orgasm began to build inside me, Kace's hands trailed down over my ass. Just like he had the night we'd fucked in the nurse's office, he used my own wetness, gathering it from where it smeared across my thighs before slipping his fingers between my cheeks to find the puckered hole there.

"Remember last time?" he murmured softly, his voice rough and tender at the same time. "Just like that. Make yourself come, Princess. Get off on Bishop's cock. Relax and let me in."

His finger penetrated the tight ring of muscle as he spoke, and the feeling of fullness made me ride Bishop with more urgency, rubbing my clit hard against his pubic bone with each stroke. Misael's hands moved over me, and when I broke my kiss with Bishop, I found him kneeling next to the couch. His lips found mine as Bishop massaged my breasts, and I rested my hands on Bish's muscled chest to support myself as I rocked up and down on his cock.

Every time Bishop buried himself inside me, Kace went deeper too, and the back and forth of feeling my core and my ass both being stretched made me groan into Misael's kiss.

I remembered the fullness of having Kace's cock in my ass, how I had balanced on a knife's edge between pain and pleasure, and my body shuddered as I imagined what it would be like to have more than his fingers inside me while Bishop fucked me from below.

"God, Cora. I can feel how much you need this. I can feel how close you are."

Bishop's hands left my breasts as he spoke, trailing down my waist to grip my hips in a firm hold, guiding my movements as I rode him harder.

He was right. I was close to coming again. My clit pulsed with every thrust of his hips, and I could feel my inner walls tightening. My updo had come partially undone, and tendrils of hair brushed against my shoulders as the four of us moved together, our bodies in perfect harmony.

When I came, my fingers curled against Bishop's chest, my nails leaving small indentations on his skin as I threw my head back. Misael nipped at my shoulder and neck as Kace added a second finger in my back hole, riding out the waves of my orgasm as he worked them both in deeper.

This time, my body barely came down from the high of the orgasm. Even as the tremors in my muscles subsided, I could feel myself building up again, wanting more.

"Now! Please!" I looked over my shoulder at Kace and saw the tension in his jaw, the beads of precum that slid down his cock, the way the muscles of his abs flexed and bunched.

Fuck, he was as ready as I was. As desperate as I was.

He didn't hesitate. He didn't make me wait or beg. He fisted his cock, spreading the glistening precum over his whole length, and I watched as he positioned himself behind me.

His face tightened in concentration and effort as the thick head breached my tight hole, and let out an involuntary noise, arching my back as my body tried to fight off the intrusion. But I wanted it. I wanted everything Kace and Bishop and Misael could give me.

The pain.

The pleasure.

Every sensation imaginable.

"With me, Coralee. Stay with me."

Misael tilted my head toward him with a gentle grip on my chin, and as Bishop pulsed into me in small strokes from below and Kace worked his way into my ass, the man beside me kissed me so deeply I could feel it all the way down to my toes.

They worked together, softening me and relaxing me, moving in sync as my body opened up to them. One of Bishop's hands shifted on my hip, and the pad of his thumb found my clit. He worked gentle, teasing circles around it, making me chase the pleasure as Kace took another inch.

Finally, I felt Kace's hips against my ass, and I broke away from Misael's kiss, gasping for breath. It didn't seem like there was room for air in my body anymore. There wasn't room for anything but the men who possessed me completely and the heart that beat only for them.

"Misael..." My voice was a throaty whisper. "Let me put my mouth on you. I want you inside me too."

He shook his head with a dazed grin, his gaze raking over my body, taking in the sight of me completely encased by his two best friends. Then he stood, his dick bobbing at the movement. He stepped closer, palming the back of my head and helping me keep my balance as I leaned forward to dart my tongue over the tip of his cock.

"Fuck," Kace grunted from behind me. "You're even tighter than before, Princess. It's better than I ever thought it would be. You're stuffed full of us."

His words lit me on fire, and I wrapped my lips around Misael's smooth mushroom head, mapping the contours of his cock with my tongue. Bishop's thumb on my clit became harder and more demanding, and liquid heat flooded my belly.

"I gotta fuck you." Kace's voice was like gravel. "I gotta move."

I nodded around Misael's cock, hoping he understood. I didn't need them to be gentle with me. My body responded to them with complete and utter trust, and I knew they would never hurt me beyond what I could take. Beyond what I craved.

And right now, I wanted to feel all three of the men I loved use me for their pleasure.

Kace drew out agonizingly slowly, and when he drove back in, I pulled more of Misael's length into my mouth, feeling his rounded head hit the back of my throat. Bishop matched his thrusts to Kace's, creating a counterpoint that made me feel like my body might burst from the overload of sensations.

"Jesus, Cora. Oh, fuck."

Misael's voice sounded tortured, and when I peered up at him through my lashes, I saw him watching the three of us, a look of raw arousal on his face.

He liked it. He liked to see his friends buried deep inside me, while I worked his cock with my lips and tongue.

Once, these boys had taken my virginity, one after the other. I had never known who was the first to be inside me, and I never wanted to know. Because it wasn't about who was first or last or in the middle.

It was about all of us, together.

Moving together.

Loving together.

My body was in such a high state of arousal that when the orgasm hit, I almost didn't realize it at first. It built and built inside me until I swore I could feel the pleasure radiating outward from my core through my entire body, infusing my limbs, making them shake like leaves.

The rhythm of my mouth on Misael's shaft faltered as my eyes rolled back in my head, and I clamped down so hard around Bishop and Kace that both men let out rough grunts.

Kace's cock throbbed in my ass, and I could feel every pulse of his length as he filled me up with his cum. Bishop went over the edge a second later, his thumb grinding against my clit as his hips jerked up into mine.

"Shit. Oh, fuck. Fuck!"

Misael's stream of curses was punctuated by a final shallow thrust into my mouth, and ropes of salty liquid spilled down my throat. I swallowed, drawing him as deep as I could and sucking until every last drop was gone.

When he finally pulled out, my jaw ached a little and his cock was slick with saliva. Slowly, Kace pulled out of me, and the two of them helped me climb off Bishop. Then we all collapsed on the couch, the three of them pulling me roughly into their laps so I was draped across all three of them. I could feel their still-hard dicks pressing against me, and I knew we needed to get cleaned up if we wanted to have any chance of making it to our wedding ceremony on time.

But my body didn't feel capable of moving.

In a minute, we'll go. Just one more minute.

I gazed up at all three of them, blinking dazedly. They were all flushed, and even though they'd just been inside me, their hands still roamed my body with possessive hunger.

Maybe it would never be sated.

In fact, I kind of hoped it wouldn't.

TWENTY-FIVE

WE WERE late to the wedding.

But I didn't give a fuck.

My parents had both decided to come, even though I knew my relationship with them would never be the same. Hell, I was sure Dad had come only to keep an eye on the criminals he was getting into bed with, already trying to find ways to spin this in his favor. But I didn't let it bother me, and I ignored the way my mom seemed afraid to touch anything, the way her lips curled back slightly as if she couldn't quite hide her disgust.

Why would I waste time on worrying about what they thought? It seemed utterly unimportant when I had a man with caramel skin and a gorgeous smile standing in front of me, his hands clasped in mine. Jo was beaming at me from where she stood off to one side, and the other two men I loved flanked Misael. Their silver rings were already settled around their fingers, a physical representation of the bond we all shared, the love that wove between the four of us like a web.

The priest who'd been hired to perform the ceremony was a friend of Claudio's, and I tried to pay attention to his words as he welcomed everyone gathered to witness our union and spoke about the sanctity of marriage. But it was hard to focus. I felt like I was falling into Misael's eyes, losing myself in their dark brown depths.

My gaze flitted from him to the other two men, and when it came time for the exchange of vows, I spoke to all three of them.

I promised to love them.

To honor and cherish them.

To stand by them no matter what may come.

And when I slid the ring on Misael's finger, I felt something shift inside me.

Months ago, when I'd been a terrified new student at Slateview High and these three men had offered me a bargain for my protection, Bishop had uttered two words that had changed my life forever.

You're ours.

Those words had become more and more true every day since then, and now they were sealed with a vow.

Bishop's lips curved up in a languid smile, and Kace's eyes burned with emotion. Misael grinned from ear-to-ear as he recited his vows, and the pure joy radiating from him seeped into my bones until I was grinning right back at him.

Then he slipped the ring on my finger, and before the priest even finished speaking the words of our marriage pronouncement, Misael kissed me. Our joined hands were trapped between us, and I could feel his fingertips clasped around the three rings he had slid on my finger.

The gathered guests applauded, and the sound was so loud and raucous that I couldn't even hear the pointed silence I was sure came from my mother and father.

Misael and I broke apart reluctantly. I had to remind myself that I could kiss him whenever I wanted now, that this was the first of many more to come—and still, my tongue darted out to touch my lips, already missing his taste.

He gave me a lopsided smile as if he could read my thoughts, threading his fingers through mine. The applause followed us as we turned and strode down the aisle, Bishop and Kace right behind us.

We burst through the doors of the church and dashed down the steps in a whirlwind. The sky was a bright blue, and even though the air was still cold, I couldn't feel it at all. Heat suffused my body, as if a fire burned low in my belly, warming me from the inside out.

When we hit the last step, Kace swept me into his arms, lifting me as if I weighed nothing.

Misael laughed, stepping forward to open the doors of the large black SUV that waited by us, driven by one of Claudio's men. We all piled inside, and although there was an empty seat up front, we ignored it entirely, shoving ourselves into the backseat. I found myself draped over the men's laps again, and Bishop gathered the material of my skirt as he closed the door.

The driver looked back at us through the rearview mirror, and I saw the glint of warm amusement in his eyes. By this time, it was no secret to anyone in Claudio's or Nathaniel's organizations that all four of us were together. Everyone knew that although my marriage was to Misael in the eyes of the law, I belonged to these three men collectively.

"Congratulations," the man said as he pulled away from the curb, and Misael caught his gaze and nodded.

I could see a change in Misael already—a seriousness in him that was another effect of our marriage arrangement. He had begun to accept his father's role in his life more fully, and I knew that one day, he would be expected to step up and lead the Vega organization. He knew it too, and I could see it in the way he interacted with the men, the way he carried himself.

He would be good at it.

He may not see it in himself yet, but I did. I could see the strength and the sweetness in him, the way he read people as if they were open books. And his easy demeanor made him the kind of person others wanted to be around, the kind they wanted to follow.

Already, Nathaniel and Claudio were making plans to move against Luke Carmine, to take advantage of his current weakness as Muse spread the word about his double-dealing. Misael and my other two men had been involved in several planning sessions, and I knew this wouldn't be the last time they would be called upon to step up and accept heavy responsibility with the two organizations.

Part of me was already worrying about them, terrified of any danger they might face, but if there was one lesson my parents had taught me—whether they'd meant to or not—it was that no amount of wealth and power could protect you from disaster.

In the end, the only thing that mattered was love.

My parents had splintered apart when their perfect life was disrupted, but I knew that would never happen with me and my husbands. We had already faced more adversity and danger than I had ever expected... but we had faced it together.

It had made us *stronger*.

As the car rolled down the street, I reached up to trail my fingertips down the side of Kace's face, watching the way his green eyes darkened at my touch. He looked so strong and masculine, with his straight jawline and muscled neck.

"I don't think your nickname fits anymore," I murmured. "The Lost Boys? It doesn't seem right, now."

He caught my hand in his and kissed my palm. "You're right. It doesn't fit."

I grinned, wriggling a little against them all as I smiled wickedly. "Right? I mean, you're definitely not boys."

Bishop laughed, his hands sliding beneath my dress to trail over my bare legs, making me shiver. Misael caressed my side, his fingertips grazing the underside of my breasts.

Kace pressed his lips against my palm again as something warm and sweet passed over his face.

"No, Coralee. We're not *lost*."

THANK YOU!

Thank you so much for reading Cora and her boys' story! Reviews make such a huge difference to authors—if you enjoyed this series, please take a second to leave a review!

You can also try my college-age bully romance, *Who Breaks First*, or my paranormal academy series, *Gift of the Gods*.

For more fun stuff, come hang out in my Facebook group, Eva Ashwood's Readers. I post giveaways, teasers, and updates there too!

Made in the USA
Middletown, DE
30 July 2021